John L. Le Conte

The Coleoptera of Kansas and Eastern New Mexico

Anatiposi

John L. Le Conte

The Coleoptera of Kansas and Eastern New Mexico

Reprint of the original, first published in 1859.

1st Edition 2023 | ISBN: 978-3-38230-706-6

Anatiposi Verlag is an imprint of Outlook Verlagsgesellschaft mbH.

Verlag (Publisher): Outlook Verlag GmbH, Zeilweg 44, 60439 Frankfurt, Deutschland
Vertretungsberechtigt (Authorized to represent): E. Roepke, Zeilweg 44, 60439 Frankfurt, Deutschland
Druck (Print): Books on Demand GmbH, In de Tarpen 42, 22848 Norderstedt, Deutschland

SMITHSONIAN CONTRIBUTIONS TO KNOWLEDGE.

THE

COLEOPTERA

OF

KANSAS AND EASTERN NEW MEXICO.

BY

JOHN L. LE CONTE, M. D.

[ACCEPTED FOR PUBLICATION, OCTOBER, 1859.]

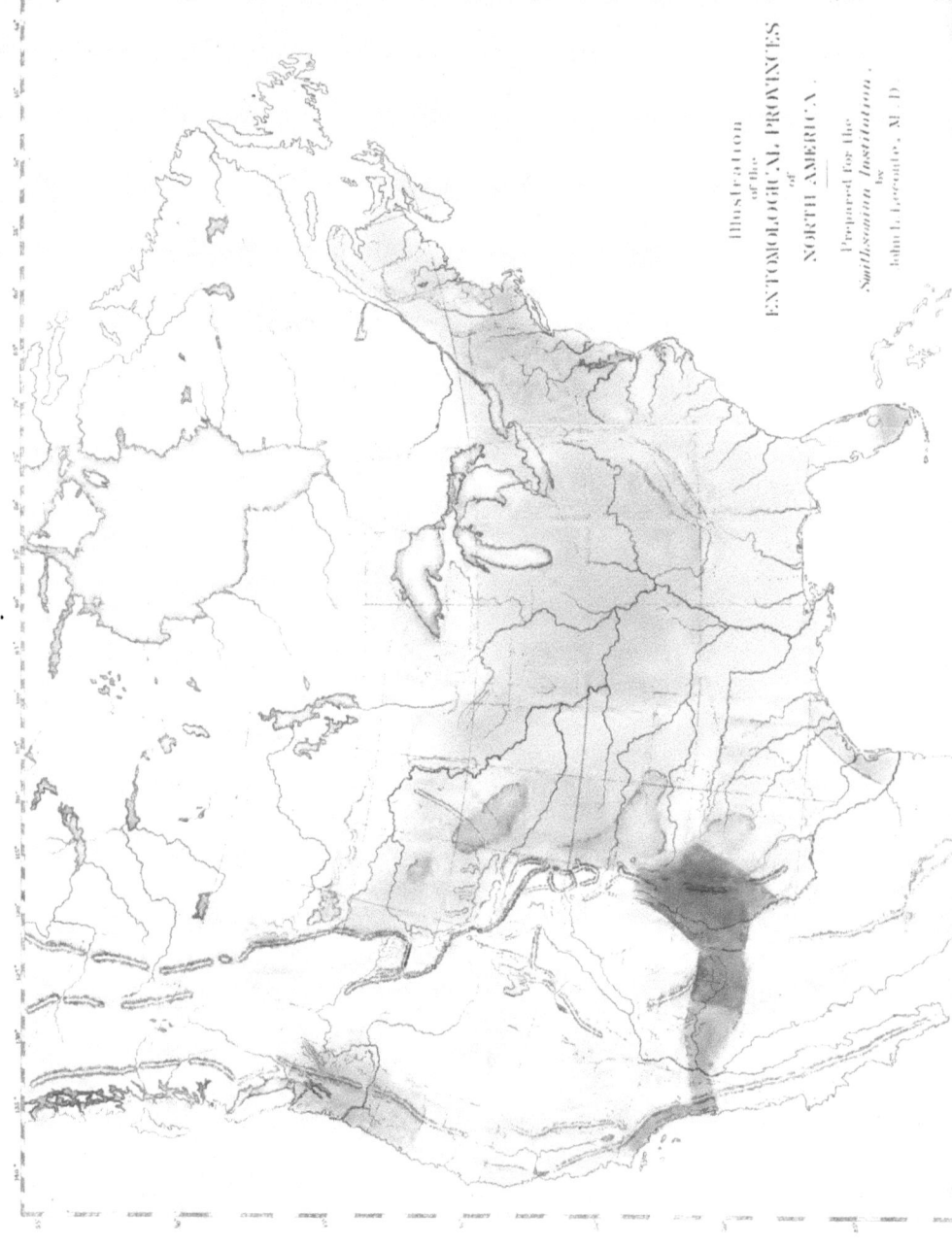

Illustration
of the
ENTOMOLOGICAL PROVINCES
of
NORTH AMERICA.

Prepared for the
Smithsonian Institution,
by
John L. Leconte, M. D.

COMMISSION

TO WHICH THIS MEMOIR HAS BEEN REFERRED.

C. ZIMMERMANN,
F. E. MELSHEIMER.

JOSEPH HENRY,
Secretary S. I.

INTRODUCTION.

THE present memoir is intended to give a catalogue of the Coleoptera thus far known to inhabit the middle eastern portion of the great central region of temperate North America. The boundaries of the province here treated of are as follows: north by the Missouri river, east by the meridian of the mouth of the Kansas or Platte river, south by about latitude 34°, and west by the main mass of the Rocky mountains.

It thus includes Kansas, a portion of Nebraska, and the eastern part of New Mexico. The eastern limit of this province is well defined; the other boundaries are indefinite, since it there fades imperceptibly into other provinces of the same great zoological district.

Before proceeding to consider the special material used in the preparation of this memoir, it will be proper to give a short sketch of the general results thus far obtained regarding the geographical distribution of Coleopterous insects in the territory of our republic.

The whole region of the United States is divided by meridional, or nearly meridional lines into three, or perhaps four, great zoological districts, distinguished each by numerous peculiar genera and species, which, with but few exceptions, do not extend into the contiguous districts. The eastern one of these extends from the Atlantic Ocean to the arid prairies on the west of Iowa, Missouri, and Arkansas, thus embracing (for convenience merely) a narrow strip near the sea-coast of Texas. This narrow strip, however, belongs more properly to the eastern province of the tropical zoological district of Mexico.

The central district extends from the western limit of the eastern district, perhaps to the mass of the Sierra Nevada of California, including Kansas, Nebraska, Utah, New Mexico, Arizona, and Texas. Except Arizona, the entomological fauna of the portion of this district west of the Rocky mountains, and in fact that of the mountain region proper, is *entirely* unknown; and it is very probable that the region does in reality constitute two districts bounded by the Rocky mountains, and southern continuation thereof.

The western district is the maritime slope of the continent to the Pacific, and thus includes California, Oregon, and Washington territories.

These great districts are divided into a number of provinces, of unequal size, and which are limited by changes in climate, and therefore sometimes distinctly, sometimes vaguely defined.

The Atlantic district may be divided into: 1, a northern province, including Maine, Eastern Canada, Nova Scotia, Newfoundland, etc., and extending westwardly from Lake Superior to Lake Winnipeg and Western Canada, which fades insensibly into the great Arctic district; 2, a middle province, limited westwardly by the Appalachian chain, and extending to Southern Virginia; 3, a western province, including Minnesota and the States of the valley of the Mississippi, as far as the State of that name; 4, a southern province, including the States south of Virginia and Kentucky; 5, a subtropical province, including the point of the peninsula of Florida; 6, a subtropical province, including the sea-coast of Texas.

The Central district, as far as known, may be thus divided: 1, a northern province, comprising the regions north of the Missouri, the plains of the Saskatchewan, etc.; 2, a middle eastern province, divided into two subprovinces, including: *a*, Kansas, and Nebraska; *b*, northeastern New Mexico; 3, a southeastern province, including Texas, with the exception of province six of the Atlantic district; 4, a southwestern province, including the upper part of the valley of the Gila; and 5, a south-southwestern province, including the lower Gila and Colorado. The unexplored portions of this district will indicate middle western, and northwestern provinces, or perhaps the necessity of constituting with them and the southwestern province a district to be called the Interior district.

The Pacific district may be divided as follows: 1, a hyperborean province, consisting of Sitka and the neighborhood; 2, a northern province, including Eastern Oregon and Washington Territories; 3, a middle province, including California, probably as far south as Santa Barbara; 4, a southern province, including California from Santa Barbara to San Diego, extending to the crest of the Sierra. Southern, or lower California is also, perhaps only in part, a province of this district;[1] but, as yet, no collections of magnitude have been received therefrom. Other provinces will, from the peculiar method of distribution of species in that portion of America, be defined when more full collections are made, but at present cannot be indicated.

At the north, the Atlantic and Central districts seem to merge imperceptibly together, about the valley of the Athabasca, and Winnepeg rivers, and finally to disappear in the limited Arctic fauna; the hyperborean province of the Pacific district also fades into this Arctic fauna, without, however, losing itself so perfectly in the northern provinces of the other districts. We have thus evidence that the American Arctic district may be divided into two provinces, an eastern and a western.

At the south, the Atlantic district merges through Florida into the Caribbean tropical province, and through maritime Texas into the Mexican lower eastern province. In the same direction the Central district merges into the Mexican upper or central province, and the Interior district, towards the Gulf of California, into the Mexican western province. Regarding the southern affiliations of the Pacific district we know absolutely nothing; scarcely a single species found at San Diego has been found in Mexico.

---

[1] A few species, collected by John Xantus, Esq., at Cape San Lucas, though all new, indicate a greater resemblance to the fauna of the lower Colorado, than to that of maritime California; this province may therefore be found eventually to belong to the interior district.

The method of distribution of species in the Atlantic and Pacific districts, as already observed by me in various memoirs, is entirely different. In the Atlantic district, a large number of species are distributed over a large extent of country; many species are of rare occurrence, and in passing over a distance of several hundred miles, but small variation will be found in the species obtained. In the Pacific district, a small number of species are confined to a small region of country; most species occur in considerable numbers, and in travelling even one hundred miles, it is found that the most abundant species are replaced by others, in many instances very similar to them; these small centres of distribution can be limited only after careful collections have been made at a great number of localities, and it is to be hoped that this very interesting and important subject of investigation may soon receive proper attention from the lovers of science on our Pacific shores.

In the Central district, consisting, as it does to a very large extent, of deserts, the distribution seems to be of a moderate number of species over a large extent of country, with a considerable admixture of local species; such at least seems to be the result of observations in Kansas, Upper Texas, and Arizona.

For the purpose of enabling these investigations to be carried on in future with less labor, I have caused the catalogues of the present memoir to be printed separately; the small size of the catalogue of species from Eastern New Mexico, will call attention to the necessity of procuring more material from that region; while the asterisks affixed to the species which have occurred in both sub-provinces, will give the results thus far obtained in geographical distribution.*

For many years in the early history of entomology in the United States, the Coleoptera of Kansas were as well known, and even more fully described than those found in the Atlantic States. They form, indeed, the subject of one of the earliest and most extensive of the valuable contributions to entomology made by Say.

Having, in the year 1845, made a journey along the Platte river to Fort Laramie, thence near the base of the mountains to the Arkansas, returning by that river and the Santa Fé road, I was enabled to follow nearly in the footsteps of Say, and had the singular good fortune to recover nearly all the species described by him, and of which the types had been destroyed to such an extent that scarcely an authentic specimen remained.

Of the species described by him, and not obtained by me from this region, I have introduced those which remain unknown to me, marking them thus (fide Say); the others I have excluded, as I possess them from Missouri, the locality in most

<hr/>

* The student will also consult in reference to the Coleopterous fauna of the Central and Pacific districts: 1. My report on the insects collected along parallel 47°, in Pacific R. R. Explorations and Surveys, vol. xi., which includes a list of the species found on the Pacific Slope, north of San Francisco; an appendix to the same in Proceedings of the Academy of Natural Sciences of Philadelphia, October, 1859.

2. Catalogue of Coleoptera of the region adjacent to the boundary line between the United States and Mexico; Journal of the Academy of Natural Sciences of Philadelphia, second series, vol. iv., No. 1.

3. Catalogue of the Coleoptera of Fort Tejon, California; Proceedings of the Academy of Natural Sciences of Philadelphia, February, 1859.

instances given by Say, and have no evidence that they are found within the region herein considered.

The results of my own labors have been measurably increased by the following collections, which I owe to the kindness of friends, and to the Smithsonian Institution :—

1. Collections brought by Lieut. Beckwith's expedition; among which were two new species; Cleonus *angularis*, and 'Cœlocnemis *punctulus* Lec. (Proc. Acad. Nat. Sc. Philad., VII, 225). The genus Cœlocnemis was not previously known east of California, where it is represented by several species; suspecting that it was collected inside of the Great Basin, I have excluded it from the catalogues here given.

2. A large number of specimens collected in Eastern Kansas, by Mr. M. Burke, and presented to me through Dr. John Torrey.

3. A very large collection made at Fort Riley, Kansas, by Dr. W. A. Hammond, U. S. A., and John Xantus, Esq.

4. Collections from the mouth of the Yellowstone river, and from the Loup Fork of the Platte, made by Dr. F. V. Hayden, and received from the Smithsonian Institution.

5. A collection made by Dr. Wm. A. Hammond, on the route from Fort Riley to Bridger's pass.

6. Similar collections made by Dr. John G. Cooper, received from the Smithsonian Institution.

The materials received from Eastern New Mexico are much more scanty, and are as follows :—

1. Four or five hundred specimens collected near Santa Fé, by Mr. Fendler, and procured for me by the kind offices of Dr. Engelmann.

2. Specimens collected by Dr. Wislizenus, on a journey from Santa Fé to Chihuahua; though few in number, these specimens were very interesting in character, and I have availed myself of the present opportunity to figure some of them, though they are possibly not found within this province of the Central district, but belong rather to the southwestern province.

3. A small, but very interesting collection made in the vicinity of Santa Fé, by the late R. C. Kern, and given me by Prof. S. S. Haldeman.

These materials were used in preparing articles for the reports of the expeditions of Capt. E. G. Beckwith, and Capt. J. Pope, U. S. A., in Pacific R. R. series, but were excluded from want of room, and are now incorporated together, with the addition of several new species since obtained from various sources.

The six provinces of the Atlantic district are marked on the map by red tints; the two provinces and two subprovinces of the Central district proper by green; the two southern provinces of the supposed Interior district by brown; and the four provinces thus far ascertained of the Pacific district by blue tints.

COLEOPTERA OF KANSAS AND EASTERN NEW MEXICO.

AMBLYCHILA SAY.

A. cylindriformis SAY, Trans. Am. Phil. Soc. IV, 409.

The specimen figured (Tab. II, fig. 1), was found by Capt. Pope on the Llano Estacado; it is very large (1·28 inches long), and in form is altogether similar to the specimen figured by me in the Proceedings of the Academy of Natural Sciences, vol. vii. p. 32. The punctures of the elytra are however much stronger, being in fact hardly smaller than those which are scattered in irregular series. The costæ of the elytra are more elevated, and the internal one extends fully to the posterior declivity. The legs are thicker, and the posterior tibiæ are entirely straight. Two other specimens were collected by Dr. Wm. A. Hammond, U. S. A., on the Platte river, about 100 miles above Fort Kearny. They agree in sculpture with the specimen from the Llano Estacado; one of them, which I consider as a male, has rather narrower elytra than the other, and has also the thorax more rounded on the sides: otherwise there is no difference between them. A larger series of specimens will indicate the nature of the strongly-marked differences of sculpture.

As confirming the correctness of the view expressed by Lacordaire regarding the identity of *A. cylindriformis* with the Californian *A. Piccolominii*, I may add, that having sent to Baron Chaudoir a figure and description of the labrum of the specimen found at Fort Union by Major Sibley, I was informed by that distinguished entomologist that he can find no appreciable difference between the figure and the labrum of the Californian specimen now in his cabinet. The figure given by M. Reiche is therefore incorrect, as already surmised.

MICRIXYS LEC.

M. distinctus, rubens, flavo-pilosus, capite thoraceque grosse punctatis, hoc transverso obovato, postice valde, angustato, lateribus valde rotundatis, elytris dorso subdepressis, striis valde cribratis, macula transversa laterali ad medium ornatis, apice summo, pedibus are antennisque piceis, his articulo 1mo rufo. Long. ·3. Tab. II, fig. 2.

Micrixys distinctus LEC. Proc. Acad. Nat. Sc. VII, 220.
Panagaeus distinctus HALD. Stansbury's Expedition to Great Salt Lake, 373.
Eugnathus ‖ *distinctus* LEC. Trans. Am. Phil. Soc. X, 375.

New Mexico: one specimen found by the late Richard Kern, Esq. This genus, unfortunately established under a preoccupied name, differs remarkably from *Panagaeus* by the head not being constricted into a neck posteriorly, and by the mandibles being thick, dilated, obtuse, and deflexed at the apex.

1

CYMINDIS Latr.

C. cribrata, nigro-picea, setis brunneis pilosella, capite thoraceque cribratim punctatis, hoc tenuiter marginato convexo, latitudine longiore, postice modice angustato et lateribus parum sinuato, angulis posticis obtusissimis, elytris cyaneo-micantibus, striis foveatim punctatis, interstitiis uniseriatim punctatis, antennis palpis pedibusque ferrugineis. Long. ·36.

Nebraska : one specimen collected by Mr. Burke. Resembles in character *C. pilosa*, but the thorax is longer, and less rounded on the sides anteriorly: the punctures of the striæ of the elytra are less closely placed, and those of the interstices almost form single rows. *C. neglecta* Hald. is smaller, and has the head almost smooth.

ANISODACTYLUS Dej.

A. chalceus, oblongus, elongatus, supra æneus, thorace latitudine vix breviore, punctulato, parce punctato, lateribus postice vix sinuatis, angulis posticis rectis, basi utrinque punctato, profundius impresso, elytris striatis, interstitiis planis alternatim parce punctatis ; subtus nigro-æneus, antennis basi rufis; tibiis anticis calcare extrorsum paulo dilatato. Long. ·37.

Santa Fé, Mr. Fendler. Allied to *A. alternans* Lec. (Ann. Lyc. Nat. Hist. 5, 184), but differs in color, and in the less dense punctuation of the alternate spaces between the striæ of the elytra.

HARPALUS Latr.

H. impotens, piceo-niger, oblongus, thorace transverso, lateribus rotundatis, margine angusto reflexo, angulis posticis rotundatis, basi utrinque vage foveato, versus angulos subdepresso, elytris ad marginem subtiliter pubescentibus, striis 2nda, 5ta, 7maque parce punctatis, interstitiis fere planis, epipleuris, ano pedibusque piceis, antennis pedibusque rufo-piceis. Long. ·38.
Lec. Journ. Acad. Nat. Sc. Philad. 2d ser. IV, 14.

One specimen found at El Paso by Dr. Thos. H. Webb. This species is narrower than *Harpalus* (*Selenophorus*) *stigmosus*, and *iripennis*, and is readily distinguished by the rounded angles of the thorax and by the elytral punctures being smaller than in the first mentioned species.

H. oblitus, oblongus, piceo-niger, nitidus, thorace latitudine sesqui breviore lateribus rotundatis, postice subangustato, angulis posticis obtusis, margine piceo postice anguste subexplanato, basi utrinque vage impresso punctulato et rugoso, elytris striis tenuibus, secunda unipunctata ; subtus, antennis palpis pedibusque ferrugineis. Long. ·5.

One male, Santa Fé, Mr. Fendler. Resembles *H. compar* Lec. (*pensylvanicus ‡* Say; *bicolor ‡* Dej.) in general appearance, but by the thorax being slightly narrowed at base, with only a few small punctures around the basal impressions, it is abundantly distinct. Fully matured specimens will probably be found to have the under surface of the body dark colored.

H. fallax, oblongus, piceo-niger, nitidus, thorace latitudine sesqui breviore lateribus rotundatis, ante medium subangustato, angulis posticis rectis subrotundatis, margine laterali postice subexplanato, cum basi tota punctulato, ad basin utrinque late foveato, elytris striis bene impressis, 2nda unipunctata ; antennis, palpis, pedibusque ferrugineis. Long. ·42.

Santa Fé: Messrs. Kern and Fendler. The elytra are slightly sinuate at tip, and those of the female are dull. This species is of the size of *H. herbivagus* Say, but the thorax is distinctly narrowed before the middle, and is much more punctured at base. A very similar nondescript species from New Jersey was kindly given me by Mr. Guex; it differs chiefly by the thorax being broader, with the sides less rounded and less narrowed anteriorly. I have named it *H. viduus*.

H. desertus, oblongus, piceus nitidus, thorace latitudine breviore, lateribus rotundatis vix explanatis, antice posticeque subangustato, angulis posticis subobtusis, subrotundatis, ad basin utrinque punctulato et foveato, elytris ad apicem obtuse rotundatis, striis bene impressis, 2uda unipunctata; antennis palpis pedibusque ferrugineis. Long. ·3.

One immature female : Mr. Fendler. Quite different from any other species known to me, although having somewhat the form of *H. megacephalus* Lec.

H. stupidus, oblongus subovalis, convexus, ater, thorace latitudine plus sesqui breviore, lateribus tenuiter marginatis antice rotundatis, postice subrectis fere parallelis, angulis posticis rectis vix rotundatis, fovea basali utrinque haud profunda, basi tota punctulata, elytris (feminæ subopacis) striis impunctatis, interstitiis vix convexis, apice sinuatis, antennis pedibusque obscure ferrugineis. Long. ·46.

One specimen from route to Fort Bridger : Mr. Drexler. More convex than *H. erythropus*, with the sides of the thorax not flattened, and the posterior angles less obtuse. From these differences in form, this species has somewhat the appearance of *H. funestus* Lec., which however has black feet, and is otherwise quite different.

DICAELUS Bon.

D. laevipennis, oblongo-ovalis, violaceo-niger, thorace antrorsum valde angustato, lateribus rotundatis, elytris tenuiter punctato-striatis, carina humerali ante medium desinente. Long. ·7. Tab. I, fig. 1.

Lec. Annals of the Lyceum of Natural History of New York, IV, 421.

Platte River Valley, near Chimney Rock. Very different from all other species yet known, by the striæ of the elytra being indicated only by rows of punctures, which are less obvious towards the apex and sides.

NOMARETUS Lec.

N. cavicollis, æneo-purpureus, nitidus, thorace obovato, postice valde angustato, sulco dorsali profundo, antice disperse punctato, postice latius concavo, profunde impresso et punctato, elytris striis utrinque 12 fortiter crenatis. Long. ·45.

One specimen, Fort Riley : Mr. John Xantus. Resembles *N. fissicollis* and *N. bilobus* (*Cychrus bilobus* Say), but differs from both by the anterior half of the thorax being covered with scattered punctures, and the posterior half being broadly concave; as in those species the posterior angles are obtuse.

CALOSOMA Fabr.

C. luxatum, nigrum subnitidum, capite subtilius punctato-rugoso, thorace capite sesqui latiore, latitudine fere triplo breviore, lateribus valde rotundatis, postice angustiore confertim punctato-rugoso, basi late rotundatim emarginato, utrinque vage impresso, elytris rotundato-ovatis, thorace latioribus, striis tenuibus rugisque transversis imbricatim insculptis, versus apicem confuse rugosis. Long. ·64—·68. Tab. I, fig. 2.

Say, Journ. Acad. Nat. Sc. of Phila. III, 149; (nec. Dej. Sp. Gen. II, 196).
Callisthenes luxatus Lec. Annals of the Lyceum of Nat. Hist. V, 200.
Carabus luxatus Lec. Ann. Lyc. Nat. Hist. IV, 445.

Platte river: on one occasion seen running on the ground in large numbers. Wider and more robust than the other North American species.

C. striatulum, nigrum, capite thoraceque nitidis leviter rugosis, hoc brevi, versus latera et basin rugoso et punctato, postice paulo angustato, ad basin late emarginato, elytris thorace latioribus, subrotundatis, dense striatis, interstitiis imbricatis, versus apicem tuberculis parvis confertis exasperatis. Long. ·65.

Milk river: one specimen found by Dr. Suckley, U. S. A., attached to the North Pacific R. R. Expedition under Gov. J. J. Stevens; Utah, Mr. Drexler. This species closely resembles *C. Zimmermanni* Lec., which is properly an Oregon species, but differs in the head and thorax being much less punctured; also in the thorax being less narrowed towards the base, and in the striæ of the elytra being more distinct.

Body black; head shining, finely but sparsely wrinkled and punctured, with the frontal impressions moderately deep. Thorax shining, about one-half wider than the head, twice as wide as its length, rounded on the sides anteriorly, obliquely but only moderately narrowed to the base, which is broadly emarginate, with prolonged basal angles; the middle of the base is, however, truncate, and not concave as in *C. luxatum ;* the sides are narrowly margined, the dorsal line is distinct; the sides are densely rugosely punctured, but the sculpture becomes indistinct on the disc. The elytra are one-half wider than the thorax, about one-fourth longer than their width, covered with close set striæ, the outer ones of which are indistinct; the interstices are transversely rugose, the rugæ being deeper at the sides and apex, so that the surface is there covered with small rounded tubercles.

ILYBIUS ER.

I. Laramacus, elongatus ovalis, antice paulo obtusus, nigro-æneus, undique subtiliter dense reticulatus, fere opaeus, elytris striola submarginali, maculaque majuscula anteapicali pallidis, ore pedibusque anterioribus piceo-rufis, pedibus posticis nigro-piceis. Long. ·37—·41.

Fort Laramie: narrower and less convex than our species found in the Atlantic States, with the sides of the thorax less rapidly converging in front: resembling more nearly in form the *I.* 4*-maculatus* of Oregon; it is, however, less oval than that species, with the sides less rounded, and the anteapical spot larger. The specific differences in this genus are very unsatisfactory, and depend entirely upon slight modifications in form, which cannot be clearly expressed in a description.

AGABUS LEACH.

A. clavatus, elongato-ovalis, modice convexus, piceus nitidus, obsolete punctulatus, capite, thoracis elytrorumque lateribus sensim rufo-piceis, pedibus antennisque ferrugineis, his articulis externis dilatatis, 9–11 nigro-piceis. Long. ·34.

Three males from Loup Fork of the Platte: Dr. Hayden. A most interesting addition to our fauna, being the analogue of *A. serricornis* of Europe. The 5th, 6th, and 7th joints of the antennæ are gradually wider; the 8th, 9th, and 10th are subrectangular, wider than long, and as wide as the 7th; the 11th is oval and pointed, narrower than the 10th.

A. griseipennis, elongato-ovalis, parum convexus, æneo-niger, supra dense (feminæ fortiter) reticulatus, elytris luteo-griseis base margineque pallidioribus, antennis palpisque flavis, pedibus ferrugineis, femoribus nigro-maculatis; thorace cum elytris angulum haud formante. Long. ·36.

Fort Laramie, one female. Differs from the species of somewhat similar color inhabiting the United States by its more elongate form, gradually tapering both before and behind; the thorax continues accurately the outline of the elytra. The reticulations are very dense, and somewhat longitudinal, especially at the base of the elytra. The Californian *A. lutosus* Lec. approaches it very closely, and it may in fact prove to be the other sex of that species, of which I possess at present only males. The form is, however, somewhat narrower.

A. obliteratus, ovalis, elongatus parum convexus, æneo-niger, nitidus supra subtilissime, vix conspicue reticulatus, elytris luteo-piceis, marginibus pallidioribus, seriebus punctorum solitis valde distinctis, ad basin thorace paulo latioribus, antennis palpis tibiis tarsisque anterioribus ferrugineis. Long. ·32.

Fort Laramie, three specimens. The sculpture of the female is hardly more conspicuous than that of the male. It is sufficiently distinguished from our other species by the characters above given.

A. spilotus, ovalis, æneo-niger nitidus, parum convexus, vix subtilissime reticulatus, thorace cum elytris angulum haud formante, elytris seriebus solitis distinctis, lineola utrinque submarginali, guttaque subapicali pallidis, antennis palpisque rufis, tarsis anterioribus rufo-piceis. Long. ·35.

Two females, Fort Laramie. Resembles *A. obtusatus,* but is less dilated, and differs very much by the reticulation being so minute as to be scarcely visible even with a high magnifier. The spots are not very obvious.

ANISOMERA Brulle.

A. cordata, supra æneo-picea, elongato-ovalis depressa, subtilissime reticulata, thorace brevi, postice angustato et lateribus sinuato, elytris thorace vix latioribus, postice non dilatatis; subtus nigra, ore antennis pedibusque rubro-piceis. Long. ·45.   Tab. II, fig. 3.
Lec. Proc. Acad. Nat. Sc. VI, 226.

Santa Fé; Mr. Fendler. Varies in having black feet; the sides of the thorax are strongly rounded in front, and subsinuate behind; the base is as wide as the apex, the anterior dilatation being produced by the curvature of the sides; the anterior angles are acute, the posterior ones rectangular. The elytra are very little wider than the thorax, regularly elongate elliptical, with the usual series of punctures becoming irregular towards the tip.

By comparing the figure here given with the South American *A. bistriata* Brullé (figured in Dejean's Icon. Col. Europe, V, tab. 23, fig. 5), it will be seen that they correspond very closely. The middle lobe of the mentum of our species is broad, short, and very obsoletely sinuate; in the generic description given by Aubé, the mentum of *A. bistriata* is said to have the middle lobe slightly prominent in the middle. This character needs confirmation, as it is hardly possible that two species so closely related should differ in this particular. Though distinct in form, this genus is separated from Agabus by very trifling differences.

SILPHA Linn.

S. bituberosa, ovalis depressa, nigra opaca, dense punctata, thorace latitudine plus duplo breviore, lateribus anguste marginatis valde rotundatis late planatis, postice utrinque late oblique impresso, elytris fortiter marginatis, apice conjunctim rotundatis, costis tribus postice paulo abbreviatis, internis duabus parum distinctis, externa tuberculum posticum transeunte. Long. ·5.

One specimen found near Fort Bridger, Mr. Drexler; belongs to the division of the genus having the 8th—11th joints of the antennæ about one-half wider than those which precede; the 8th to 10th are not much wider than long; the 2d is quite as long as the 3d.

S. truncata, oblonga, atra subopaca, capite thoraceque dense aciculato-punctatis, hoc antrorsum valde angustato, ad basin trisinuato, postice utrinque versus latera oblique impresso, elytris lateribus fortius marginatis, subtilius punctatis, ad dodrantem callo discoideo parum distincto utrinque notatis, ad apicem late truncatis; antennarum articulo 3io vix longiore. Long. ·5—·67. Tab. 1, fig. 3.

Say, Journ. Acad. Nat. Sc. III, 193. Lec. Proc. Acad. Nat. Sc. VI, 278.

Platte river, near the Forks. A very distinct species; the specimen figured is a male: the abdomen of the female projects far beyond the elytra.

CARPOPHILUS Leach.

C. apicalis, oblongus, piceo-niger, minus subtiliter punctatus et flavo-pubescens, thorace modice convexo, latitudine haud sesqui breviore, lateribus marginatis rotundatis, elytris thorace sesqui longioribus, rufis, circa scutellum et ad apicem extrorsum oblique infuscatis, pedibus antennisque testaceis. Long. ·1.

Platte river: found also in Georgia; narrower and more convex than is usual in this genus.

C. carbonatus, oblongus subdepressus, piceo-niger, parcius pubescens et punctatus, thorace latitudine plus sesqui breviore angulis omnibus rotundatis, ad apicem vix emarginato, lateribus late rotundatis tenuiter marginatis, elytris alutaceis obsoletius punctulatis, thorace duplo longioribus, antennis basi piceis. Long. ·1.

Found on the Platte river and at Lake Superior.

MELIGETHES Kirby.

M. ruficornis, oblongus subconvexus, nigro-viridis, dense subtiliter punctatus, breviter cinereo-pubescens, thorace antrorsum angustato, lateribus rotundatis anguste marginatis, pone medium subfoveatis, angulis posticis subrectis, antennis tarsis tibiisque rufis, his anticis subtiliter serratis, posterioribus latioribus ultra medium et ad apicem ciliatis; unguibus simplicibus, prosterno postice anguste rotundato. Long. ·11.

Platte river, not rare. Differs by obvious characters from all European species thus far described, and were it not that the prosternum is rounded posteriorly, it would enter Erichson's division B, (Ins. Deutschl. 173.)

M. sævus, oblongus subconvexus, niger, dense subtiliter punctatus, breviter cinereo-pubescens, thorace antrorsum angustato, lateribus rotundatis anguste marginatis, angulis posticis rotundatis, margine basali undulato, antennis basi piceis; tibiis anticis 5-dentatis ad basin serratis, intermediis extrorsum emarginatis et posticis dense spinulosis; unguibus simplicibus, prosterno postice late rotundato. Long. ·11.

One specimen; Platte river; belongs to Erichson's division C, (loc. cit. 179.)

AND EASTERN NEW MEXICO. 7

HISTER Linn.

H. instratus, quadrato-ovalis, niger nitidus, thorace bistriato, lateribus dense flavo-ciliatis, elytris stria suturali utrinque abbreviata, tribus externis integris, marginali brevissima, rudimentalique ad basin interna notatis, macula utrinque lunata maxima rubra ornatis; tibiis anticis bidentatis, posticis compressis biseriatim spinulosis, femoribus posticis majoribus rubro-tinctis. Long. ·24—·32.

Platte river: Intermediate between *H. arcuatus* Say, and *H. biplagiatus* Lec., having the elytral spot and compressed posterior tibiæ as in the latter, while by the very densely ciliate margin of the thorax, the thick and sometimes reddish posterior thighs, and the more numerous spines of the posterior tibiæ it is evidently related to the former. The outer series of spines is composed of numerous spines placed irregularly in nearly a double row, while in *H. biplagiatus,* they are distant and regular; the posterior tibiæ are slightly less compressed than in that species.

H. nubilus, rotundato-ovalis, niger, nitidus, thorace bistriato, stria externa margini approximata, ante medium abbreviata, elytris striis externis 4 integris, 5ta postica brevi, suturali ante medium antice abbreviata, epipleuris striis duabus punctatis, striolaque brevi inferna; mesosterno fere truncato; pygidio sat dense punctato, tibiis anticis sub-5-dentatis. Long. ·25.

One specimen: Platte river. This and the next are very distinct from any of our other species, in which the mesosternum is not distinctly emarginate, and the elytral marginal striæ wanting.

H. pollutus, rotundato-ovalis, niger nitidus, thorace bistriato, stria externa margine approximata ante basin abbreviata, elytris striis externis 3 integris, 4ta ad medium postice abbreviata, 5ta obsoleta, suturali utrinque parum abbreviata, epipleuris 3-striatis; mesosterno fere truncato; pygidio parcius punctato, tibiis anticis sub-4-dentatis. Long. ·20.

Kansas and New Mexico.

SAPRINUS Leach.

S. spurcus, quadrato-rotundatus, æneo-niger, nitidus, capite punctulato, thorace lateribus dense punctatis, antice vix obsolete impresso, margine laterali sublævi, elytris striis dorsalibus æqualibus ad medium abbreviatis, interna cum suturali integra connexa, marginali brevi obliqua cum humerali fere juncta; punctatis postice subaciculatis, spatio scutellari quadrato, margineque laterali lævibus, epipleuris bistriatis punctatis, tibiis anticis sub-6-dentatis. Long. ·14.

One specimen: Platte river. Belongs to my division 4 (Proceedings Acad. Nat. Sc. Phila. VI, 40), having the head not margined in front, the epipleuræ bistriate, the prosternum transversely convex, with an anterior fovea on each side, and the prosternal striæ parallel, abbreviated in front. It is closely related to *S. lugens*, but is very considerably smaller, with the punctures of the elytra less aciculate, the thorax scarcely impressed, and with the punctures of the sides not extending to the lateral margin, which is only punctulate.

S. parumpunctatus, rotundatus, nigro-æneus nitidus, parce punctulatus, thorace lateribus et basi confertim punctato, antice haud impresso, elytris striis paulo pone medium abbreviatis, æqualibus, 4ta cum suturali integra conjuncta, marginali brevi, postice haud dense punctato, pedibus rufis, tibiis anticis denticulatis. Long. ·13.

One specimen: Platte river. Resembles *S. conformis,* and *placidus,* but differs, besides slighter characters above mentioned, by the punctures of the posterior portion of the elytra being smaller and less deep. Belongs to my group 6, having the prosternum transversely convex, foveate each side in front, with the striæ remote and divergent ; the head not margined in front, and the epipleuræ bistriate.

S. pratensis, rotundatus, nigro-æneus, vel nigro-cupreus, nitidus, thorace lateribus et basi confertim punctato, antice haud impresso, elytris striis ad medium abbreviatis æqualibus, 4ta cum suturali conjuncta, marginali brevi, dimidio postico dense punctatis, extrorsum fere aciculatis, punctis inter striam humeralem et 2udam ad basin, extensis ; pygidio dense punctato, pedibus rufis, tibiis anticis denticulatis. Long. ·13—·20.

Platte river, and Fort Riley, abundant. I was inclined to believe this to be *S. orbiculatus* Marseul found in Texas, but the punctures extending to the base are not entirely outside of the dorsal striæ, but occupy also the spaces as far as the 2d stria ; these spaces are sometimes also slightly rugous. The prosternum is subcarinate, margined with the striæ divergent ; it therefore belongs to my division 7, (Proc. Acad. VI, 40)

PHILEURUS LATR.

P. valgus. (Tab. II, fig. 4.)

On comparing specimens from Georgia, Missouri, Texas, and New Mexico, forming *P. castaneus* Hald., with one from Brazil in the collection of the Academy of Natural Sciences, I can perceive no difference whatever. Burmeister has observed that the species extends its range from South America into Mexico, but adds that he has not seen specimens from the regions north of that country. Individuals occur of a dark brown color, but I suspect these to be immature : the usual color is a full black.

POLYPHYLLA HARRIS.

P. decemlineata, picea, dense luteo-squamosa, clypeo maris valde concavo, antice latiore recte truncato (feminæ lateribus parallelis apice sinuato), capitis lateribus albopilosis ; thoracis canaliculati vittis tribus, scutello medio, elytrorum sutura vittis utrinque tribus humeralique brevi cum externa confluente niveo-squamosis ; subtus niveo-squamosa, pectoribus longe luteo-villosis, pedibus ferrugineis parcius squamosis (tibiis anticis maris bidentatis, feminæ tridentatis). Long. 1·0—1·4. Tab. I, fig. 6, (*a*, tib. ant. feminæ.)

Lec., Proc. Acad. Nat. Sc. VII, 218 ; Journ. Acad. Nat. Sc., 2d ser. III, 230.

Melolontha 10-*lineata* SAY, Journ. Acad. Nat. Sc. III.

Kansas, New Mexico, Texas, California, Oregon. The thorax has occasionally a round whitish spot near each side.

THYCE LEC.

T. squamicollis, ferrugineo-picea, capite thoracequc confertissime punctatis, pilis depressis squamiformibus pallidis obsitis, elytris nitidis punctatis et rugosis, brevissime parce pubescentibus, pygidio abdomineque squamulosis, pectore valde lanuginoso. Long. 1·03. Tab. II, fig. 5.

Lec. Journ. Acad. Nat. Sc. 2d ser. III, 232.

One female found at Albuquerque, by Dr. T. Charlton Henry, U. S. A. Reddish brown above and beneath ; head densely punctured, front nearly straight anteriorly, with the margin broadly reflexed, covered with small pale yellowish scales. Thorax convex, narrowed in front, much rounded and subserrate on the sides, broadly but feebly channelled in the middle, vaguely impressed each side near the anterior angles which are acute; densely punctured, covered thinly with yellowish scales like those on the head; scutel densely pubescent with a medial glabrous line. Elytra shining, not densely punctured, with rugæ as in most of the species of *Phyllophaga*; each puncture furnished with a pale short hair. Pygidium densely, abdomen sparsely covered with small pale scales. Pectus with dense long yellow hair. Anterior tibiæ three-toothed; middle and posterior tibiæ with two sharp teeth near the middle.

LACHNOSTERNA Hope.

L. lanceolata, picea (mas oblonga, femina crassa), supra squamulis lutescentibus dense tecta haud punctata, clypeo reflexo vix emarginato, thorace lateribus antice valde rotundatis, angulis posticis rectis, linea dorsali subglabra, elytris vittis utrinque tribus indistinctis subglabris; subtus dense sordide pubescens, antennis pedibusque obscure ferrugineis. Long. ·53—·68. Tab. 1, fig. 5(♀).

Lec. Journ. Acad. Nat. Sc. 2d ser. III, 237.

Melolontha lanceolata Say, Journ. Acad. Nat. Sci. III, 242.

Tostegoptera lanceolata Blanch. Cat. Col. Mus. Paris, 149 ; Burm. Lamell. II, 2d, 356.

Ancylonycha lanceolata Lacordaire, Gen. Coleopt.. III, 285.

Throughout Kansas, extending into Eastern New Mexico and Upper Texas. The male is winged, while the female is apterous. The genus *Tostegoptera*, as very properly observed by Lacordaire (Gen. Col. III), does not differ from Lachnosterna by any essential characters.

DIPLOTAXIS Kirby.

D. obscura, oblonga nigro-picea, subnitida, capite hemihexagono, dense punctato, antice late emarginato, margine anguste reflexo, sutura frontali profunda, vertice late bifoveato, thorace brevi dense punctato, medio paulo latiore, lateribus rotundatis, angulis anticis subacutis, posticis subrectis, margine laterali reflexo, ad angulos latiore impresso, elytris punctatis, tricostatis, tibiis anticis tridentatis. Long. ·45.

One specimen from the Black Hills : Dr. Hammond. Resembles somewhat *D. brevicollis* Lec., but is more densely punctured, with the sides of the thorax more rounded, and more deeply impressed at the angles: the two foveæ of the vertex, if a constant character, will serve easily to distinguish it.

DIAZUS Lec.

Corpus oblongum alatum, breviter pubescens; caput mediocre, clypeo marginato, hemihexagono, sutura frontali parum distincta ; labrum transversum late emarginatum; palpi maxillares articulo ultimo elongato-ovali, acuto haud impresso; mandibulæ vix prominulæ obtusæ; mentum quadratum antice concavum ; antennæ breves, 9-articulatæ, clava parva triphylla. Tibiæ anticæ unicalcaratæ, 3-dentatæ; posteriores paulo incrassatæ, obsolete bicoronatæ, calcaribus parvis; tarsi antici tibiis haud longiores, intermedii tibiis paulo longiores, postici tibiis breviores, crassiusculi; articulis omnium 4 primis æqualibus, 5to paulo longiore, unguiculis haud dentatis. Thorax linea apicali nulla, margine membranaceo distincto.

A genus belonging to the *Diplotaxes*, and having the characteristic form of abdomen of that tribe, viz., the 5th ventral segment united without suture to the propygidium, with the spiracle each side midway between the anterior and posterior margin. It differs, nevertheless, remarkably from the other genera by the nine-

2

jointed antennæ and simple ungues. The rough sculpture and short sparse pubescence give the insect very much the appearance of an *Ochodæus*.

D. rudis, ferrugineo-fuscus, oblongus, parum nitidus, pilis brevibus minus subtilibus, albidis minus dense vestitus, capite punctato, hemihexagono, clypeo antice latius emarginato, thorace convexo antrorsum angustato, lateribus valde rotundatis, dense punctato, elytris rugose punctatis, sutura costisque solitis tribus parum elevatis, pygidio confertim punctato. Long. ·30.

Two specimens from the black hills: Dr. W. A. Hammond. The punctures are large and not deep. The body beneath is more shining, and less densely punctured.

OMORGUS Er.

O. scutellaris, apterus, niger, thorace cataphracto valde inæquali, lateribus rotundatis, elytris seriatim minus distincte punctatis, transversim cœlatis, interstitiis subquadratis, subæqualiter parum elevatis. Long. ·6—·65. Tab. I, fig. 4.

Lec. Proc. Acad. Nat. Sc. VII, 214.

Trox scutellaris Say, Journ. Acad. Nat. Sc. III, 238.

From Platte river to Santa Fé. Other nearly allied species found in Texas are described by me in the place above cited; from all of them, however, it may be distinguished by the assemblage of characters here given.

CANTHON Illiger.

C. praticola, subovatus, ater opacus, supra subtilius licet evidenter granulatus, clypeo 6-dentato, dentibus duobus mediis obtusis, reliquis latis modice prominulis, thorace brevi convexo, lateribus valde rotundatis, elytris capite thoraceque vix longioribus, basi late emarginatis, lateribus et apice rotundatis, planiusculis versus scutellum paulo impressis, striis parum distinctis; thorace subtus versus angulum anticum tuberculo minuto marginali instructo, pro receptione pedum parum excavato, pygidio convexiusculo, parce subtiliter granulato. Long. ·27—·37.

Kansas and New Mexico. Resembles *C. nigricornis*, but the form is less abbreviated, the lateral teeth of the clypeus are more prominent, the elytra are less sparsely granulate, and the pygidium is more finely granulate, not impressed or carinate towards the base.

For the purpose of enabling the relations between the species of *Canthon* inhabiting the United States to be understood, as well as of providing names for several nondescript species, I add the following synoptic table :—

A. Prothorax pleuris linea transversa a coxis procedente obsoleta vel nulla.

a. Prothorax pleuris margine versus angulum anticum tuberculo minuto subinterrupto.

  * Clypeo rotundato, bidentato ; (species magnæ).

       rotundatus supra granulatus, oculis latiusculis   *vigilans.*

       rotundatus, oculis angustissimis ;

            supra evidenter granulatus   *lævis.*

            obsolete granulatus   *chalcites.*

  ** Clypeo 6-dentato; (species minores).

    § Pygidio rude granulato, basi plus minus carinato ;

            clypei dentibus omnibus magnis ;

            oblongo-rotundatus, supra rude granulatus   *ebenus.*

            rotundatus, supra subtilius granulatus   *depressipennis.*

            clypei dentibus lateralibus minus prominulis ;

            breviter rotundatus, supra subtiliter, elytris parcius granulatus   *nigricornis.*

§§ Pygidio vix granulato, haud carinato;
　　ovato-rotundatus, supra granulatus　　　　　　　　　　　　*praticola.*
　　rotundatus, supra haud granulatus　　　　　　　　　　　　*abrasus.*
b. Prothorax pleuris margine versus angulum anticum tuberculo nullo (pro receptione
　　pedum parum concavis).
* Clypeo 6-dentato, dentibus externis parum prominulis;
　　rotundatus, ater, granulis depressis parcis obsitus　　　　　*simplex.*
** Clypeo 4-dentato, dentibus internis acutis;
　　rotundatus, nitidus, nigro-cyaneus, punctulatus　　　　　　　*cyanellus.*
B. Prothorax pleuris linea transversa a coxis procedente notatis, antice pro receptione
　　pedum subito declivibus; (clypeus dentibus internis obtusis reliquis obsoletis).
　　thorace punctato, elytris subopacis (cupreus, vel viridis)　　*viridis.*
　　thorace fortius punctato, elytris nitidis punctulatis　　　　*perplexus.*

The species in the above synopsis, not before mentioned, are:—

C. depressipennis. A black, or greenish black species found in Georgia, resembling very closely *C. ebenus*, and only differing from that species by the body being less oblong, the thorax less suddenly rounded on the sides, and the granulations of the upper surface more minute. Long. ·30—·35.

C. abrasus. A small rounded dull black species, from Georgia, with the eyes broader than usual, having no visible sculpture on the head and thorax, and very feebly granulate on the elytra, which are depressed in the scutellar region: the striæ are very indistinct, the pygidium not granulate. Long. ·24.

C. cyanellus. A shining, very dark blue rounded species found in Texas, and given me by Mr. Ulke, having the clypeus oblique on the sides, and 4-dentate in front, the middle teeth being narrower than in the other species; the thorax is very minutely punctulate, much rounded and almost angulated on the sides, with a fovea remote from the margin opposite the widest part; the elytra are feebly punctulate, obsoletely striate, impressed at the scutellar region. Pygidium dull, obsoletely punctulate. Margin of the prothorax beneath without the small tubercle usually seen near the anterior angle. Long. ·37.

Synonyms to be observed are:—

C. lævis: Scarabæus lævis Drury, Oliv.; *Scarabæus volvens* Fabr.; *Ateuchus volvens* Fabr.; *Scarabæus pilularius* ‡ De Geer. *Coprobius obtusidens* Ziegler, is a slight variety of this species.

C. viridis: Copris viridis Beauv.; *Onthophagus viridicatus* Say. *Ateuchus obsoletus* Say, is a copper-colored variety of this species, which is more frequently found on leaves than in any other situation. Chevrolat (Ann. Ent. Soc. France, 2d ser. X, 632) refers Beauvois' species to *Onthophagus*, but I do not see anything in the figure or description to warrant such a reference.

Ateuchus probus Germ., Ins. Nov. 98, probably belongs to this genus, but I do not know any species that agrees with the description.

MELANOPHILA Escн.

M. **miranda,** nigra, ænescens, subtiliter dense punctulata, capite guttis quinque politis, circulo positis, thorace guttis quatuor anticis (intermediis maioribus), altera utrinque pone medium, lineaque dorsali postica nitida lævigatis; elytris margine basique tenuiter rubris, lineisque flavis decussatis ornatis. Long. ·65. Tab. II, fig. 7.

Lec. Trans. Am. Phil. Soc. XI, 212.
Phænops mirandus Lec. Proc. Acad. Nat. Sc. VII, 83.

One specimen found at Fort Union, by Major Sibley. This is the most elegant species of the genus, the name of which seems by no means appropriate, yet being older than that of *Phænops* must be retained.

CHRYSOBOTHRIS Esch.

C. quadrilineata, fusco-ænea, punctata opaca, latiuscula, capite pubescente, thorace lineis quatuor elevatis nitidis, medio valde canaliculato, elytris utrinque lineis elevatis nitidis, marginali suturalique integris, hac antice latiore, intermediis duabus confluentibus et pone medium interruptis. Long. ·48—·60.

Lec. Trans. Am. Phil. Soc. XI, 233.

Santa Fé: Mr. Fendler. Broader and more robust than the other species found in the United States, and easily known by the sculpture of the thorax. The latter is twice as wide as its length, very deeply channelled in the middle, with a broad shining sparsely punctured entire vitta each side of the channel, and another each side which does not reach the apex; the depressed portions are opaque and very densely punctured. The elytra are wider than the thorax, serrate at the sides and apex, with an entire elevated shining line near the suture, dilated anteriorly so as to reach the suture, and an entire slender elevated line parallel with the outer margin; between these are two elevated lines which are confluent in two places, and interrupted behind the middle; the base is very deeply foveate as usual: the depressed portions are all densely punctured, and without lustre. Body beneath coarsely punctured, prosternum flat, covered with long white hair, with a slightly elevated smooth medial line.

C. cuprascens, obscure cupreo-ænea, longiuscula, minus depressa, fronte viridiæneo, dense punctato pubescente, thorace irregulariter punctato, vage impresso et subcanaliculato, elytris confertim punctatis, utrinque biimpressis, lineis nitidis elevatis, suturali marginalique integris, discoidali interna bis interrupta, externa ad medium postice abbreviata. Long. ·31.

Lec. Trans. Am. Phil. Soc. XI, 234.

One specimen: Mr. Fendler. Resembles some of our smaller species, but is more convex and more coppery. The posterior impression of the elytra is deeper and larger than the anterior one, and although slightly lobed is not sinuous; the elevated lines are nearly smooth. The anterior tibiæ of the male are slightly bent, and armed with a tooth internally near the tip.

PSILOPTERA Solier.

P. Woodhousei, ænea, nitida, chalybeo-variegata, thorace confertim punctato, brevi, lateribus valde rotundatis, antrorsum angustato, angulis posticis rectis, elytris apice integris, seriatim crenatis, maculis irregularibus opacis transversis profunde impressis. Long. ·72—·97. Tab. II, fig. 6.

Lec. Trans. Am. Phil. Soc. XI, 195.
Dicerca? *Woodhousei* Lec. Proc. Acad. Nat. Sc. VI, 68.
Var. major, *Psiloptera valens* Lec. Proc. Acad. Nat. Sc., 1858, 66.

Creek Boundary Expedition : Dr. S. W. Woodhouse ; Texas, Mr. Schott.

Body coppery bronze, varied with bluish reflections, moderately stout and convex; head strongly punctured, with three faint confluent elevated lines on the front;

labrum green; thorax cribrate punctate, more than twice as wide as broad as long, narrowed in front, very strongly rounded on the sides, narrowed a little towards the posterior angles, which are rectangular and sharp. Elytra with rows of large punctures, and with numerous deep impressed subconfluent spaces, which are opaque, densely punctured and finely pubescent; tip entire. Legs green bronzed, knees, tip of the tibiæ, and tarsi steel blue. Tip of the abdomen very slightly truncate in the male, rounded in the female.

CHAULIOGNATHUS Hentz.

C. basalis, elongatus niger, thorace fulvo nitido, subrotundato, marginato, disco plus minus nigro, elytris rugose punctatis, flavo-fulvis macula magna communi triangulari basali, trienteque postico nigris, abdomine flavo, sæpe nigro annulato, articulo ultimo nigro. Long. ·42.

Abundant near Fort Bridger and in the Black Hills: Dr. Hammond, Mr. Drexler. Varies much in the size of the black spot of the thorax, which is sometimes emarginate, and sometimes even divided into four dots. The antennæ of the male are as long as the body, of the female two-thirds as long. The thorax in *C. limbicollis* and *scutellaris* is opaque, while in the present it is very smooth and shining.

NIPTUS Boieldieu.

N. ventriculus, rufo-piceus, nitidus, pube sordida minus subtili dense vestitus, thorace globoso, grosse punctato, postice valde coarctato, tuberculis parum elevatis quatuor transversim positis, e pilis efformatis; elytris ovalibus, ventricosis, seriatim punctatis, setis erectis sat dense hispidis. Long. ·10.

Santa Fé: Mr. Fendler. The elytra are twice as wide as the thorax, and about one-half longer than wide; the punctures are tolerably large and distant, and become smaller on the declivous posterior portion. The second joint of the antennæ is as long as the third.

TRYPOPITYS Redt.

T. punctatus, elongatus, fuscus sericeo-pubescens, thorace ad basin utrinque transversim excavato, et in medio breviter carinato, elytris striis e punctis digestis vix impressis. Long. ·25.

One specimen: Mr. Fendler. Precisely resembles in appearance *T. sericeus*, (*Xyletinus sericeus* Say, Journ. Acad. Nat. Sc. V, 171), but the thorax is less deeply excavated at base, and the striæ instead of being deep and cribrate are hardly impressed, and the interstices are flat.

PACTOSTOMA Lec.

P. anastomosis, piceus, pilis sordidis setiformibus parce vestitus, thorace punctato, subcanaliculato, latitudine breviore lateribus rotundatis marginatis, basi subtruncato, angulis posticis obtusis, elytris ovalibus postice subacutis et declivibus, parce punctatis, sutura, margine costisque tribus acute elevatis, quarum prima recta, secunda et marginali flexis cum prima confluentibus, tertia irregulari utrinque valde abbreviata. Long. ·42—·5. Tab. II, fig. 11.

Lec. Journ. Acad. Nat. Sc. 2d Ser. IV, 19.

Microschatia anastomosis Lec. Proc. Acad. Nat. Sc. VI, 446.

Asida anastomosis Say, Journ. Acad. Nat. Sc. 3.

Pelecyphorus anastomosis Lec. Ann. Lyc. Nat. Hist. V, 129.

Ologlyptus anastomosis Lac. Gen. Col. V, 159.

Kansas and New Mexico, near the Rocky mountains. The first dorsal costa is nearly straight, and extends from the base to the apex; the second commences near the base, and being curved, unites with the first about one-third from the tip; the third is irregular, running from the anterior third to the posterior fourth ; the marginal one is entire, and unites with the first near the tip.

ASIDA Latr.

A. opaca, oblonga atra, opaca, brevissime parce flavo-pubescens, capite thoraceque scabro-punctatis, illo antice transversim excavato, hoc antrorsum angustato, latitudine breviore, lateribus rotundatis late subdepressis postice subsinuatis, angulis omnibus acutis, posticis paulo productis, elytris parce subtiliter minus profunde punctatis vage inæqualibus, nonnunquam obsolete sulcatis, lateribus marginatis, humeris obtusis. Long. ·5—·68. Tab. I, fig. 9.

Say, Journ. Acad. Nat. Sc. III, 254.

Euschides opaca Lec. Annals of the Lyceum of Nat. Hist. V, 127.

Kansas and New Mexico, near the mountains : specimens from the latter locality are smaller, and have the elytra much more uneven than those found near Platte river, but do not appear sufficiently distinct to be considered as another species.

EUSCHIDES Lec.

E. convexa, nigra subnitida, capite punctato antice transversim sulcato, thorace latitudine sesqui breviore, subtiliter parce punctato, lateribus rotundatis, margine punctato anguste reflexo, angulis anticis acutis, posticis obtusis haud rotundatis, elytris transversim convexis, pone basin thorace paulo latioribus, ad apicem valde declivibus, subtiliter rugosis lineis tribus obsoletis utrinque notatis, humeris marginatis prominulis. Long. ·85. Tab. I, fig. 10.

Arkansas river, near the mountains. Nearly allied to *Eu. obovata* Lec.; but with the thorax more convex and less broadly margined, and the elytra less obovate and more convex transversely. From *Eu. convexicollis* Lec. it differs by the larger and more strongly margined thorax.

PELECYPHORUS Solier.

P. sordidus, picco-niger, capite modice transversim impresso, punctato, thorace latitudine fere sesqui breviore ante medium angustato, lateribus rotundatis subserratis deplanatis et subreflexis, confertim grosse inæqualiter punctato, elytris oblongo-ovalibus, convexis postice subacutis, sutura margine costisque utrinque duabus elevatis, lineis transversis sinuatis inter se irregulariter connexis; prosterno postice late sulcato. Long. ·75—·85. Tab. I, fig. 11(♀).

Lec. Proc. Acad. Nat. Sc. VI, 446.

Arkansas river, near the mountains: also found in New Mexico, by Dr. Webb, of the Mexican Boundary Commission. In the female, the elytra are twice as wide as the thorax, and more rounded on the sides than in the male. The specimens are covered with a yellowish earthy substance which adheres closely.

EUSATTUS Lec.

E. reticulatus, rotundatus convexus, ater opacus, thorace obsoletissime punctulato, lateribus marginatis paulo reflexis, angulis posticis valde productis, elytris foveis quadratis vagis impressis, obsolete sulcatis, tibiis anticis extrorsum serrulatis, versus apicem lævibus. Long. ·46—·53. Tab. I, fig. 7 (*a*, tibia antica).

Lec. Ann. Lyc. of Nat. Hist. V, 132.

Zophosis reticulata Say, Journ. Acad. Nat. Sc. III, 250.

Found near the Rocky mountains from Platte river to Santa Fé, and westward as far as Tucson. Larger than *E. convexus* Lec., and less convex; the sides of the thorax are not suddenly depressed behind the middle as in that species.

EMBAPHION Say.

E. contusum, atrum opacum, thorace latitudine fere duplo latiore, antice profunde emarginato, lateribus valde rotundatis, disco parce punctato, parum convexo, margine late explanato modice reflexo, angulis anticis subacutis, posticis latis obtusis valde rotundatis, ad basin medio recte truncato, elytris dorso planis, postice valde declivibus et acute angustatis, thorace vix latioribus, fortiter reflexo-marginatis, seriatim subtilius sat dense muricato punctatis, ad apicem singulatim breviter acuminatis (♀), vel in cauda brevi prolongatis ( ). Long. ·55—·65. Tab. I, fig. 8. Lec. Journ. Acad. Nat. Sc., Philad., 2d ser. IV, 40.

Fort Laramie and Santa Fé. Though differing very much in form from the Helæus like *E. muricatum* Say, the forms of the antennæ, oral organs and legs require it to be associated with that species. The figure given saves the necessity of a long description, while the diagnosis above will enable the species to be readily recognized.

Two specimens found by Dr. Webb, near the Mexican boundary, differ in having the sides of the thorax much more strongly reflexed, so that that part becomes much narrower than the elytra. This is, probably, merely a local variety, as similar differences occur among individuals of *Cychrus elevatus*, and in many other insects which have the margins of the body widely reflexed.

BLAPSTINUS Latr.

B. pratensis, elongato-ovalis convexus, ater opacus, breviter subtiliter fusco-pubescens, capite thoraceque punctatissimis, hoc latitudine sesqui breviore, lateribus late rotundatis, ad apicem emarginato, angulis anticis acutis ad basin sinuato, angulis posticis rectis, elytris striis fortius punctatis, interstitiis paulo convexis, punctulatis. Long. ·20—·23.

Platte River Valley, abundant. Differs from the Californian *B. pubescens* Lec., by the finer pubescence, by the more widely rounded sides of the thorax, and by the more prominent anterior angles.

B. vestitus, elongato-ovalis, convexus, æneo-niger, pube albida minus subtili dense vestitus, capite thoraceque confertim punctatis, hoc latitudine vix breviore, antrorsum paulo angustato, lateribus late rotundatis, ad apicem emarginato, angulis anticis acutis, ad basin sinuato, angulis posticis rectis, elytris striis punctatis, interstitiis planis punctulatis. Long. ·20.

Two specimens from Platte River Valley. Very closely allied to the preceding, but the coarse pubescence, and the flattened intervals of the elytra seem to be sufficient characters for separating it.

CENTRONOPUS Solier.

C. opacus, elongatus, niger opacus, capite postice punctato, fovea verticali notato, antice concavo, epistomate late rotundato et fortiter marginato, thorace quadrato, antice vix angustiore, lateribus parum rotundatis, angulis posticis acutis, parum convexo, parce punctato, elytris striis e punctis parvis constitutis. Long. ·57.

One male; Black Hills, Dr. Hammond. Differs from the Mexican *C. suppressus*, according to description, by being opaque, with finer elytral striæ. The sexual characters are nearly as in that species; the anterior femora have on the anterior face near the base an oval patch of yellow hair; the tibiæ are dilated internally at the middle into an obtuse angle, then broadly emarginate to the tip, at the inner side of which is a dense short brush of yellow hair; the first three joints of the anterior and middle tarsi are dilated, and furnished beneath with a dense brush of yellow hair; the middle tibiæ are thick internally at the apex and have also a brush of hair.

XYSTROPUS Solier.

X. pinguis, ater opacus, subtilissime punctulatus, brevissime pubescens, thorace brevi, lateribus valde rotundatis, basi sinuato, angulis posticis haud prolongatis, elytris striatis, interstitiis paulo convexis. Long. ·37.

Santa Fé, Mr. Fendler: one specimen. Resembles *X. brevis* (*Cistela brevis* Say), but differs in the antennæ and feet being entirely black. The thorax is less deeply sinuate at the base, and the posterior angles are less acute, and not prolonged.

CYSTEODEMUS Lec.

C. vittatus, niger, capite thoraceque opacis, vage grosse punctatis, illo ad basin fere truncato, hoc subquadrato, subtiliter canaliculato, ad basin valde emarginato, elytris brevibus, inflatis obtusis, cribrato-punctatis, vitta angusta rubra abbreviata ornatis, abdomine amplissimo lævigato. Long. ·5—·7. Tab. II, fig. 9.
Lec. Proc. Acad. Nat. Sc. VI, 330.

New Mexico, Dr. Wislizenus: found on the journey from Santa Fé to Chihuahua.

C. wislizeni, cyanescens, nitidus, capite thoraceque grosse punctatis, illo postice rotundato, hoc pentagono, canaliculato, angulis lateralibus acutis, elytris splendide cyaneis, sphericis, foveis profundis confertis cancellatis. Long. ·45—·65. Tab. II, fig. 10.
Lec. Ann. Lyc. Nat. Hist. of New York, V, 158; Proc. Acad. Nat. Sc. VI, 330.

Drs. Wislizenus and Webb, found in the same region with *C. vittatus.*

MORDELLA Fabr.

M. insulata, longiuscula, nigra, capite thoraceque cinereo haud dense pubescentibus, hoc latitudine breviore, lateribus late rotundatis, elytris pube nigra indutis, sutura basique cinereo-marginatis, vitta obliqua a humero ad quadrantem extensa, maculaque transversa pone medium dense cinereo-pubescentibus; subtus maculis lateralibus cinereo-pubescentibus, antennis thorace longioribus basi, tibiis tarsisque anticis fusco-testaceis, stylo anali elongato. Long. ·18—·21.

Two specimens, from Fort Riley; Mr. John Xantus. Approaches *M. oculata* Say, more nearly than any other species, but is readily distinguished by the markings as above described; the oblique vitta from the humerus does not reach the suture; the scutellum is densely clothed with cinereous hair.

MORDELLISTENA Costa.

M. æmula, elongata, parallela, nigra, pilis pallide sericeis obsita, elytris evidenter punctulatis, pedibus posticis, tibiis carinulis numerosis brevibus obliquis, tarsorum articulo 1mo tibia vix breviore, 5-carinulato, 2d bicarinulato. Long. ·18.

One specimen: Platte river. Elongate, not attenuated behind, black, above and beneath with gray silvery hair; head and thorax very finely punctulate, the latter scarcely wider than long, somewhat narrowed in front, slightly rounded on the sides, bisinuate at the base, with the middle lobe broadly rounded. Elytra more than three times as long as the thorax, parallel on the sides, obtusely rounded behind, distinctly punctulate. Anal style slender. Posterior tibiæ broad, with six or seven very short oblique ridges on the supero-external margin; first joint of posterior tarsi not shorter than the tibia, with five similar oblique ridges; second joint with two.

M. divisa, fusco-nigra, supra dense helvo-pubescens, elongata, postice subattenuata, capite thoracoque ante medium rufo-testaceis, elytris evidenter punctulatis; pedibus posticis, tibiis carinulis 2 vel 3 minutis obliquis, tarsorum articulo 1mo tibia haud breviore carinulis 4, 2ndo duabus instructo; antennarum basi pedibusque anterioribus rufo-testaceis, unguiculis simplicibus. Long. ·11.

Platte river: resembles *M. marginalis* (*Mordella mary.* Say), but differs by the pubescence being coarser, more abundant, and of a yellowish brown color. The thorax is a little wider than long, not narrowed in front, broadly rounded on the sides, feebly bisinuate at base; the anterior half, with the head is reddish yellow, and the outline separating the yellow from the black is sinuate as in the species above mentioned.

In thus introducing the present genus into the fauna of the United States, a few remarks regarding our numerous species of *Mordellidæ* will be appropriate. The genera which they represent are five in number, and may be thus separated:—

A. Scutellum quadratum, transversum postice subemarginatum   *Tomoxia* COSTA.
B. Scutellum triangulare, apice rotundatum;
   a. Palpi maxillares articulo ultimo valde dilatato securiformi   *Glipa* LEC.
   b. Palpi maxillares articulo ultimo triangulari;
     Antennæ articulis externis valde transversis, velutinis   *Sphalera* LEC.
     Antennæ articulis externis triangularibus, haud transversis;
     Pedes postici simplices   *Mordella* LINN.
     Tibiæ tarsique postici carinulis notati   *Mordellistena* COSTA.

To *Tomoxia* belong *M. bidentata* Say, and a nearly allied smaller species.

To *Glipa* belongs only *M. hilaris* Say. The body is slender; the outer joints of the antennæ triangular; the maxillary palpi elongated, with the last joint in the form of an obtuse isosceles triangle, attached by its apex. The middle tibiæ are longer than the tarsi; the posterior tibiæ only moderately dilated, longer than the first joint of the tarsi, and destitute of oblique ridges; the anal style is short, truncate and submarginate.

Sphalera is the genus indicated, but not named by Lacordaire (Gen. Col. V, 609, note). The only native representative known to me is *M. melæna* Germ.

To *Mordella* belong *Anaspis 4-punctata* Say; *M. 8-punctata* Fabr.; *oculata* Say; *insulata* Lec.; *serval* Say; *Anaspis triloba* Say; *M. marginata* Mels.; *lineata* Mels.; *scutellaris* Fabr. (*atrata* Mels.); *undulata* Mels., and four nondescript species.

To *Mordellistena* belong all the other species described by Say, Melsheimer, and myself; natural groups among them may be easily formed by the number and position of the tibial ridges, and the arrangement of the colors of the upper surface. *M. sericans* and one nondescript are remarkable by the posterior tibiæ having a fine carina extending along the upper edge, and only a single very long oblique ridge on the outer surface.   These species do not indicate a generic separation, however, and represent the European *M. testacea*, the type of *Stenalia* Muls.

OPHRYASTES Sch.

O. vittatus, niger, albido-squamosus, rostro trisulcato, sulco medio profundissimo, lateralibus rectis profundis, mox ante oculos abbreviatis, thorace latitudine plus duplo breviore inæquali, parce profunde punctato, lateribus sub-bituberosis, canaliculato, sæpe fusco trivittato, elytris striis vix impressis, profunde punctatis, sutura cuprascente fusca, interstitiis 3io, 5to et 7mo fusco vittatis. Long. ·41—·48. Tab. I, fig. 13(♂). (*a.* rostrum).

SCHÖNHERR, Cure. 1,509; 5,819. LEC. Proc. Acad. Nat. Sc. VI, 443.

Liparus vittatus SAY, Journ. Acad. Nat. Sc. III, 316.

Platte and Arkansas rivers; found also at Eagle Pass, Texas.   The elytra of the male are but little wider than the thorax; those of the female are more rounded, slightly flattened on the back, and about one half wider than the thorax.   The dark vittæ of the thorax and elytra appear to be produced partly by abrasion, as specimens occur in which they are hardly to be seen; but the suture as far as the first stria is covered with brown scales having a coppery reflection.

CLEONUS Sch.

C. lutulentus, ater densissime sordide pubescens, vix variegatus, capite cum rostro grosse disperse punctato, hoc longitudinaliter vage impresso, medio vix carinato, thorace varioloso antrorsum angustato, lateribus antice rotundatis, disco paulo obscuriore, elytris inæqualibus, punctis magnis striatim positis. Long. ·37—·43 (sine rostro).

Santa Fé, Mr. Fendler.   Smaller and stouter than *C. trivittatus* Say, with the thorax more densely variolate, and hardly perceptibly excavated or carinated; the elytra have three or four vague impressions, not seen in that species.

C. pulvereus, alatus, niger sordidus, rostro carinato, cum capite vage grosse punctato, fronte foveata, thorace latitudine haud longiore, lateribus breviter tubulato, angulis anticis rotundatis, grosse punctato ad basin medio late foveato, lateribus dense albo-pubescentibus, elytris convexis, oblongis postice obtuse rotundatis, striis fortiter punctatis haud impressis, totis dense albo-pubescentibus, lineis tribus curvatis obliquis sub-denudatis utrinque notatis; subtus albo-pubescens, obscuro variegatus. Long. ·5.

Arkansas river, one specimen.   Of the same size and shape as *C. vittatus* Say, but very distinct by the thorax being not narrowed gradually in front, and not carinate, as well as by the different color.

C. angularis, niger, rostro carinato, cum capite fortiter vage punctato, fronte late foveata, thorace quadrato, lateribus subsinuatis, pone apicem valde constricto et ad apicem tubulato, angulis pone apicem rectis extantibus, varioloso-punctato, ad basin medio profunde foveato, elytris oblongis convexis, cribrato-striatis, interstitiis cinereo-pubescentibus spatiis denudatis variegatis, alternis cum sutura elevatis; subtus cinereo-pubescens, vix nebulosus. Long. ·36—·45. Tab. I, fig. 12.

Two specimens: collected by Lieut. Beckwith.   The first joint of the funiculus of the antennæ is slightly elongated, the others are short; the species, therefore, belongs to the division (called genus by Schönherr) Pachyeraerus.   The projecting anterior angles of the thorax are very remarkable.

DEROBRACHUS Serville.

D. geminatus, piceus, nitidus, thorace valde transverso, antice non angustato, parce punctulato, lateribus quadrispinoso, spina antica minore, elytris fere lævigatis, margine angustiore reflexo. Long. 2·9. Tab. II, fig. 12 (femina).
Mas minor (long. 1·5—2·25), antenuis longioribus crassioribus (fig. 12 *a*), pedibus anticis punctis elevatis exasperatis.
Lec. Proc. Acad. Nat. Sc. VI, 223.

New Mexico and Texas. The only female yet obtained was collected at Albuquerque, by Dr. T. C. Henry; several males were afterwards found by Messrs. Schott and Clark, of the Boundary Commission, at various places in Texas.

PRIONUS Geoffroy.

P. curvatus, piceus, thorace subtiliter parce punctulato, spina anteriore tenui valde acuta, media hamata, angulis posticis subrectis prominulis, elytris subtiliter parce punctulatis et rugosis, spina suturali distincta ; oculis magnis, antennis 12-articulatis. Long. 2·06.

One female from near Santa Fé. Resembles nearly *P. californicus* Motsch. (*crassicornis* Lec.), but the anterior spine of the thorax is more slender, and the middle one is curved backwards; the elytra are somewhat less punctured and rugose, but this is not a good character, as judging from a large series of *P. californicus*, it seems subject to variation.

P. fissicornis, nigro-piceus, nitidus, thorace subtiliter parce punctato, lateribus obtuse tridentato, elytris thorace latioribus parce sat grosse punctatis, obsolete costatis. Long. 1·0—1·6. Tab. I, fig. 14 (mas).
Mas antennis crassissimis valde imbricatis 27—30-articulatis, articulis subtus valde incisis (*a*).
Femina antennis tenuibus imbricatis, 25-articulatis, articulis subtus sinuatis (*b*).
Haldeman, Proc. Acad. Nat. Sc. III, 125 ; Lec. Journ. Acad. Nat. Sc. 2d ser. II, 108.

Platte river, New Mexico, and Texas, not rare.

P. emarginatus, piceus, nitidus, thorace punctatissimo, flavo-piloso, antrorsum angustato, lateribus ante medium unispinoso, angulis posticis rectis, elytris grosse parcius punctatis ; antennis 14-articulatis. Long. ·75. Tab. II, fig. 13 (mas).
Mas antennis crassis valde imbricatis, articulis 3—13 ad apicem subtus valde emarginatis. Femina latet.
Say, Journ. Acad. Nat. Sc. III, 327 ; Lec. ibid. 2nd ser. II, 107.

Kansas and New Mexico, near the Rocky Mountains.

CRIOCEPHALUS Muls.

C. asperatus, piceus tenuiter pubescens, thorace subtransverso, lateribus obtuse angulatis, dorso plano ad latera granulis parcis exasperato, utrinque profunde lunatim excavato, medio subcanaliculato, ad basin fovea mainscula impresso, elytris thorace parum latioribus, subtiliter rugosis, lineis utrinque duabus elevatis ; oculis modice prominulis, genis subacutis ; antennis corporis dimidio vix longioribus, versus basin crassiusculis, articulis ultimis quatuor subito brevioribus. Long. ·96.

Kansas and New Mexico. Differs from *C. agrestis* by the more flattened thorax, with more numerous elevated granules, and distinctly angulated sides. The antennæ are also heavier, and do not differ remarkably in length in the two sexes, and their joints from the eighth to the eleventh are each one-half shorter than the seventh.

DRYOBIUS Lec.

D. sexfasciatus, supra niger nitidus, capite thoraceque flavo-pubescentibus, illo inter antennas glabro transversim elevato, hoc fascia nigra ad medium ornato, latitudine paulo breviore, postice leviter coarctato, punctato, callis tribus dorsalibus notato, ante medium transversim impresso; elytris fasciis tribus apiceque late flavo-pubescentibus; subtus flavo-fasciatus, antennis pedibusque rufis, illis articulis internis subtus longe fimbriatis. Long. ·65—1·0. Tab. I, fig. 15 (femina).
Lec. Journ. Acad. Nat. Sc. 2d ser. II, 23.
Callidium sexfasciatum Say, Journ. Acad. Nat. Sc. III, 415.

Alabama (Prof. Haldeman) and Ohio (Dr. Kirtland): Say found it on the Arkansas river. The antennæ of the female are but little longer than the body, those of the male are one-half longer. The femora are compressed and gradually slightly clavate.

ARHOPALUS Serv. (emend. Lec.)

A. charus, niger subtilissime punctulatus, thorace latitudine sesqui breviore, flavo-pubescente, fasciis tribus angustis nigris, elytris ad apicem oblique intus truncatis, a basi ad quadrantem flavis, gutta utrinque parva ad medium, fascia lata pone medium apiceque flavis, antennis pedibusque nigris. Long. ·85. Tab. I, fig. 16 (var.).
Lec. Journ. Acad. Nat. Sc. 2d ser. I, 17; Proc. Acad. Nat. Sc. VI, 68.
Clytus charus Say, Bost. Journ. Nat. Hist. I, 193.

Missouri, Dr. Engelmann; Creek Boundary, Dr. Woodhouse. The segments of the body beneath are edged with yellow; the humeri are marked with a black dot; the apical yellow spot sometimes includes a black spot, as in the specimen figured. I have seen only females of this species.

STENASPIS Dup.

S. solitaria, atra supra glabra, subtus parce cinereo-pubescens, thorace latitudine fere duplo breviore, parce punctato, ante basin callo lævi alteroque utrinque versus latera modice elevatis, lateribus ipsis bituberculatis, elytris subtilissime strigosis, parce subtiliter punctulatis, pedibus cyanescentibus. Long. 1·43. Tab. II, fig. 14 (femina).
Lec. Proc. Acad. Nat. Sc. VI, 441.
Cerambyx solitarius Say, Journ. Acad. Nat. Sc. II, 410.
Callichroma solitarium Hald. Trans. Am. Phil. Soc. X, 32.
Smileceras solitarium Lec. Journ. Acad. Nat. Sc. 2d ser. II, 9.

New Mexico, Dr. Wislizenus; Kansas, Say; Texas, Messrs. Clark and Schott; Tucson, myself. The male has the antennæ longer than the body and slender.

TYLOSIS Lec.

T. maculatus, niger, thorace elytrisque coccineis, illo latitudine fere duplo breviore, punctato, callis quinque lævibus nigris, elytris confertim punctatis, macula humerali, alterisque utrinque tribus nigris. Long. ·75. Tab. II, fig. 15.
Lec. Journ. Acad. Nat. Sc. 2d ser. II, 9.

New Mexico, Dr. Wislizenus (probably found west of Santa Fé). The humeral spot of the elytra in one specimen is obsolete. The antennæ of the male are much longer than the body.

ACMAEOPS Lec.

A. dorsalis, elongata, nigra opaea, supra parce breviter cinereo-pubescens, capite thoraceque confertissime punctatis, hoc latitudine subbreviore, convexo antice posticeque constricto, lateribus valde rotundatis, subcanaliculato, linea dorsali tenui lævi, elytris thorace latioribus superallelis, punctatis, vitta subsuturali lutea postice sensim attenuata, et pone medium abbreviata, apice rotundatis, subtus cinereo-pubescens, epimeris dense pubescentibus. Long. ·45.

One specimen, from Republican Fork of Kansas river, kindly given me by Dr. T. B. Wilson. The antennæ are slender and reach two-thirds the length of the elytra; behind the middle of the elytra and extending nearly to the apex is a very obsolete yellowish stripe, which in other specimens may be found to be well developed, in which case there would be on each elytron a subsutural vitta abbreviated behind, and an external one abbreviated in front.

Resembles in appearance some of the varieties of *A. marginalis* Lec. (? *Leptura longicornis* Kirby), but the thorax is more robust and more rounded on the sides, the legs are entirely black, and the apex of the elytra more rounded.

LEPTURA Linn.

L. cribripennis, atra breviter parce pilosa, capite dense, thorace grosse punctato, hoc convexo, lateribus late rotundatis, utrinque constricto, elytris rubris subglabris, cribratim punctatis, ad apicem nigricantibus et intus oblique truncatis bidentatis, dente exteriore longiore; articulis antennarum 4, 5, 6, 9 et 10mo basi pallidis, 6to et 8vo pallidis macula apicali parva nigra notatis. Long. ·7.

One specimen found by me on Platte river. Very nearly allied to *L. cinnamoptera* Kirby, but the elytra are much more coarsely punctured, and the lower half of the fourth joint of the antennæ is pale, while in the latter species there is merely a small pale spot at base.

MONILEMA Say.

M. appressum, nigrum, thorace lateribus non spinosis, antice posticeque parce punctatis, elytris ante medium parce punctatis, dorso antice planis, lateribus subito valde declivibus. Long. ·97.
Tab. II, fig. 17.
Lec. Journ. Acad. Nat. Sc. 2d ser. II, 168.

New Mexico: one specimen: Dr. Wislizenus. Differs from the other species known to me by the flattened back and suddenly deflexed sides of the elytra.

STENOSTOLA Muls.

S. saturnina, plumbeo-nigra, undique cinereo-pubescens, thorace latitudine haud longiore, punctato, lateribus subrotundato, pilis subtilibus erectis brevibus parce vestito, versus basin densius pubescente, elytris punctis remotis postice subtilioribus, ad apicem singulatim rotundatis. Long. ·5.

One specimen from Kansas, kindly communicated to me by Mr. Burke. From its color it resembles at first sight *Saperda moesta* and *concolor*, but the short convex front and dentate ungues will at once remind the student of the generic differences. Of the usual smooth thoracic spots seen in the species of this genus, only two very faint ones remain; they are situated about the middle, equidistant from each other and from the side.

AMPHIONYCHA Lec.

A. ardens, minus elongata cylindrica, atra, pube nigra erecta vestita, capite fronte vittisque duabus postice divergentibus lææte flammeo-pubescentibus, thorace supra flammeo-pubescente, vitta dorsali atra, latitudine sesqui breviore, lateribus parum sinuatis, elytris thorace paulo latioribus grosse punctatis, margine laterali ad humeros latiore, et ad dodrantem extenso ornatis. Long. ·35.

Fort Riley: John Xantus, Esq. Broader than *A. flammata*, and readily distinguished by the thorax being one half broader than its length, with the lateral vittæ much wider.

Also allied to these two is a third species found in Northern New York, and in New Hampshire; for specimens of it I am indebted to Mr. Henry Ulke, it may be thus characterized:—

A. subarmata, minus elongata cylindrica, atra, pube nigra erecta vestita, capite flammeo-pubescente, thorace latitudine vix breviore, lateribus sinuatis, medio tuberculo acuto prominulo armatis, vitta angusta sublaterali flammeo-pubescente, elytris grosse punctatis juxta suturam late sulcatis, sutura magis elevata. Long. ·26—·28.

ÆDILIS Serv.

Æ. spectabilis, niger subtiliter dense cinereo fuscoque pubescens, thorace fusco maculis albis confluentibus utrinque ornato, elytris basi fasciisque tribus undulatis obliquis fuscis (intermedia latiore) notatis, pedibus fusco-annulatis, antennis longissimis cinereis, articulis 1—5 subtus dense pubescentibus, apice fuscis, 5to fasciculo apicali recurvato interno ornato. Long. ·91. Tab. II, fig. 16.

Lec. Proc. Acad. Nat. Sc. of Philadelphia, VII, 82.

Fort Union: one specimen: Major Sibley. The figure renders unnecessary any farther description of this beautiful species.

LEMA Fabr.

L. trivirgata, elongatula, parallela, testacea nitida, antennis (articulo primo excepto) thoracis maculis duabus (capitisque lateribus, abdominisque maculis sæpe), tibiarum apice tarsisque nigris; thorace latitudine longiore, medio valde coarctato, antice grossius parce punctato; elytris fortius punctato-striatis, interstitiis postice haud elevatis, vitta suturali alteraque submarginali angustis nigris. Long. ·31.

Santa Fé: Mr. Fendler. Similar in appearance to *L. trilineata*, but known at once by the larger punctures of the thorax and elytra. The thorax is also more deeply constricted at the middle, and the outer vitta of the elytra is always narrower, usually extending only from the 9th to the 10th stria; in one specimen this vitta is interrupted behind the humerus. In another the second and third joints of the abdomen are marked each with a medial transverse black spot, and the occiput and two posterior spots of the head are black.

COSCINOPTERA Lac.

C. franciscana, oblonga, antice angustior, postice vix attenuata, nigra, subtus densius, supra sat dense albido-tomentosa, thorace latitudine sesqui breviore, lateribus obliquis parum rotundatis, punctato, linea angusta dorsali lævi, elytris fere dense punctatis, labro flavo-marginato. Long. ·18—·20

Fort Riley: Mr. Xantus. Closely related to *C. dominicana*, but differs by the pubescence of the upper surface being much more dense, and by the elytra being more densely punctured. The sexual characters are as in that species.

CRYPTOCEPHALUS Geoffr.

C. mucoreus, cylindricus, niger nitidus, subtus dense, supra subtiliter cinereo-pubescens, thorace convexo, subtiliter sat dense punctato, spatio parvo dorsali lævi, elytris basi marginoque ultra medium late coccineis, maculaque coccinea rotundata apicali utrinque ornatis, punctis magnis striatim digestis, interstitiis parce subtiliter punctatis. Long. ·25.

Fort Riley, one specimen: Mr. John Xantus. It has also been received from Texas by Mr. Ulke. A very distinct species; the elytral markings are a broad basal band curving along the margin to beyond the middle, and a small apical spot. Some of the varieties of *C. notatus* are similarly marked, and it is quite possible that the present species will be found also to vary in this respect.

PARIA Lec.

P. opacicollis, pallide flava, thorace latitudine fere duplo breviore, valde convexo, alutaceo sub-opaco, parce subtiliter punctulato, lateribus late rotundatis, elytris antice fortiter postice subtilius striatim punctatis, nitidis, margine postice, sutura, maculisque 4 sæpe nigris. Long. ·13.

Fort Laramie: a very pretty species, readily distinguished by the faint sculpture of the thorax. The spots are placed, an oblong one at the middle of the base, and a larger quadrate one at the middle nearer the side than the suture.

P. pumila, saturate rufo-testacea, nitida, thorace convexo, quadrato, antice paulo angustato, lateribus parum rotundatis, parce punctato, elytris convexis, punctis paucis striatim positis ad basin majoribus, postice fere lævibus; antennis nigris, ad basin pedibusque flavis, pectore nigro. Long. ·10.

One specimen sent me by the late A. Melly, Esq., as coming from Kansas. The striæ consist only of a few distant large punctures towards the base, which become rapidly smaller and indistinct behind.

HETERASPIS.

H. nebulosa, cuprea, pube longa albida irregulariter vestita, capite inter oculos profunde angu-latim impresso, fronte canaliculata, occipite bifoveato, thorace irregulariter punctato, latitudine haud longiore, ad basin truncato, lateribus rotundatis, elytris thorace latioribus convexis, striis grosse punctatis haud impressis postice obsoletis, interstitiis alutaceis. Long. ·15—·19.

Kansas, near Fort Laramie. The genus *Heteraspis* belongs in the vicinity of Eumolpus, and is distinguished from the other native genera by the following assemblage of characters:—

The mouth and eyes are not protected by the thorax, which beneath is simply truncate; the head is marked with a deep impression between the eyes; this impression is angulated each side, and continues around the inner posterior and inferior part of the eyes, forming a kind of orbit. The ungues are armed with a long acute tooth in *H. pubescens* Mels.; with a short acute tooth in *H. curtipennis* Mels., and in the next species, while in the one here described the tooth is almost obsolete.

H. smaragdula, viridi-ænea, parce albo-pubescens, capite profunde angulatim impresso, fronte vix canaliculata, thorace latitudine haud longiore, lateribus rotundatis, ad basin late rotundato, punctato subrugoso versus apicem sublævi, elytris longiusculis, convexis, thorace latioribus, striis haud impressis antice punctatis postice obsoletis, interstitiis alutaceis parce punctulatis. Long. ·20.

One specimen found at Fort Laramie.

MYOCHROUS.

M. squamosus, longiusculus, piceo-æneus, dense griseo-squamosus, breviter pubescens, capite thoraceque confertissime punctatis, hoc subrotundato, lateribus haud dentatis, elytris thorace non latioribus, punctis subquadratis striatim positis, postice obsoletis; tibiis anticis intus subarmatis, femoribus posticis haud dentatis; antennis versus basin rufis. Long. ·18.

Platte river, under dried buffalo excrement. Differs abundantly from *M. denticollis* by the absence of serration on the sides of the thorax, as well as by the posterior femora being not armed with a tooth; the scales of the upper surface of the body are broad.

The genus *Myochrous* consists of elongated pubescent Eumolpi, in which the thorax is slightly lobed behind the eyes; the latter are small and prominent; the antepectus is excavated for the reception of the head; the claws of the tarsi are not perceptibly toothed. The anterior tibiæ are armed with a more or less prominent denticle on the inner surface near the middle; the posterior femora are sometimes simple, and sometimes toothed.

ŒDIONYCHIS LATR.

Œ. lugens, elongato-ovalis, atra opaca, thorace elytrisque anguste marginatis, illo disperse punctato,, ad basin late rotundato, abdominis segmentis dorsalibus pallidis. Long. ·21.

Santa Fé, Mr. Fendler. Of the same shape, but smaller than *Œ. concinna* (*Haltica concinna* Fabr.), and easily known by its dull opaque black color, and by the base of the thorax not being sinuate near the posterior angles. The elytra appear impunctured; the pale color of the dorsal surface of the abdomen shows a little beneath at the margin and tip.

Œ. lobata, pallida, thorace angulis anticis acutis, lateribus late reflexis, elytris nigro-piceis subtiliter punctatis, basi versus scutellum latius, margine laterali trilobato, maculisque utrinque duabus disci pallidis, sutura anguste pallescente; subtus fusco-testacea, pedibus pallidis. Long. ·20.

One specimen from Kansas river. Allied to *Œ. quercata*, but larger, and with the elytra less broadly margined; the arrangement of the colors on the latter is also very different.

HALTICA ILLIGER.

H. punctigera, oblongo-ovalis, pallide flava, thorace latitudine duplo breviore, punctulato, lateribus rotundatis marginatis, dorso convexiusculo, punctis 4 nigris notato (externis sæpe deficientibus), elytris dense subtiliter punctatis, sutura, vitta discoidea apicem haud attingente, alteraque juxta marginem nigris, tibiarum apicibus, tarsis antennisque fuscis, his articulis tribus primis subtus flavis. Long. ·30.

Kansas, near the Rocky mountains. Belongs with a numerous series of species allied to *H. alternata;* it is broader than that species, the thorax is more convex and more rounded on the sides; and the elytra are finely, but strongly and densely punctured.

H. pluriligata, pallide flava, elongata, thorace latitudine sesqui breviore, fere obsolete punctulato, guttis nigris quatuor, lineolaque dorsali versus basin ornato, lateribus rotundatis marginatis, elytris subtiliter parce punctulatis, sutura, vitta discoidea apicem haud attingente, alteraque juxta marginem nigris; tibiis ad apicem, tarsisque fuscis, antennis nigro-piceis, articulis tribus primis flavis supra infuscatis. Long. ·32.

Kansas and Texas. Also allied to *H. alternata*, but narrower and with a less transverse thorax. Both this and the preceding, as well as the next species belong to Chevrolat's division (called genus by some authors) *Disonycha*.

H. cervicalis, ovalis, pallide flava, capite, antennis, pedibus, elytrisque nigris, his punctulatis subalutaceis; thorace subtilius marginato, levi. Long. ·2.

Kansas and Georgia. Very similar to *H. collaris*, but rather stouter than that species, and distinguished by the uniform pale-yellow color of the under surface.

H. semicarbonata, ovalis convexa, fusco-atra, elytris opacis subtiliter punctatis, thorace parce punctulato, flavo, ad basin versus angulos posticos rectos sinuato, clypeo, abdominis segmento ultimo ventrali, coxis femoribusque flavis; antennarum articulis 1—3 subtus, tibiisque posticis ad basin flavis. Long. ·24.

Santa Fé: one specimen : Mr. Fendler. Belongs to the division named *Disonycha* by Chevrolat, and resembles in appearance *H. collaris* Fabr., but is broader, having the form of *H. cervicalis*; it is readily distinguished from both by the dull elytra and different arrangement of the colors beneath.

H. ambiens, elongata, convexa, cyanea nitida, thorace virescente, punctulato, ad basin late rotundato, ante basin profunde transversim sulcato, sulco versus angulos profundiore, elytris subtiliter punctulatis, carina submarginali distincta, postice curvata et versus suturam obliterata. Long. ·22.

Santa Fé: Mr. Fendler. Differs from *H. subplicata* in the smaller size, and by the more elevated submarginal costa of the elytra being curved behind. It nearly resembles a nondescript species from New Hampshire (*H. alni* Harris), but the thorax is more convex, and the elytra more deeply punctured, while the curved portion of the costa is less prolonged towards the suture; in both the elytra are broadly sulcate about the middle, just within the costa.

H. subplicata, elongata, obscure cyanea, parum nitida, thorace latitudine paulo breviore, subtiliter punctulato, lateribus rectis angulis omnibus distinctis, postice fortiter transversim sulcato, elytris parce punctulatis, plica submarginali minus elevata versus apicem sensim obliterata notatis. Long. ·25.

One specimen : found in Platte river valley. Belongs to a numerous group of the division *Graptodera* Cherv., having an elevated fold parallel with the outer margin of the elytra ; this fold in the other species is, however, much more elevated and curved posteriorly towards the suture.

H. punctipennis, elongata, læte viridi-ænea, thorace antrorsum angustato, latitudine sesqui breviore, lateribus late rotundatis, vix subtiliter punctulato, postice transversim tenuiter obsolete sulcato, elytris thorace paulo latioribus, distincte licet subtiliter punctatis, antennis nigris. Long. ·2.

Kansas and Santa Fé. Specimens from New Mexico were collected by the late Richard C. Kern, Esq., and were given to me by Prof. S. S. Haldeman. This is a *Graptodera* of slender form, and is readily distinguished by the distinctly punctured elytra, and by the slight posterior impression of the thorax.

H. obliterata, elongata, chalybeo-atra subopaea, thorace subtiliter punctulato, ad basin late rotundato, ante basin stria transversa subtili impresso, elytris subtiliter fere obsolete punctulatis. Long. ·27.

One specimen, Mr. Fendler. Very distinct from other species of *Graptodera* known to me, by the fine transverse line of the thorax being obliterated towards the sides.

H. torquata, elongata, thorace punctulato ad basin late rotundato, ante basin profunde transversim sulcato, plus minusve cupreo, elytris chalybeis purpureo micantibus, confertim punctulatis, margine laterali cupreo-æneis; subtus obscure ænea, pedibus purpureo-chalybeis. Long. ·2.

Santa Fé, Messrs. Fendler and Kern. An elongate *Graptodera* distinguished by the color and the fine dense punctuation of the elytra, from all the species that resemble it.

H. bitæniata, elongata nigro-picea, supra pernitida, capite postice pallidiore, thorace fusco-testaceo, maculis tribus obscuris, parce punctulato, ante basin transversim leviter impresso, et in medio foveato, elytris punctulatis nigris, vitta lata dorsali margineque (mox ante apicem sæpe connexis) pallidis; antennis pedibusque fusco-testaceis, femoribus posticis obscuris. Long. ·18—·21.

Santa Fé, Mr. Fendler. Larger than *H. elongata* Fabr. (*tæniata* Say), and with it, belongs to the division *Systena* Chevr. The marginal and dorsal vittæ sometimes unite near the tip.

LONGITARSUS Latr.

L. nigripalpis, elongata, alata, flavo-testacea, oculis palpisque nigris, fronte cariuata, vertice tuberculis duobus parum elevatis, linea impressa definitis, thorace latitudine breviore, lateribus rotundatis, valde convexo, alutaceo, ante basin transversim sulcato, elytris thorace latioribus oblongis, subtiliter punctulatis pone basin late impressis; tibiis posticis elongatis haud sulcatis, calcari parvo terminatis. Long. ·12.

One specimen, Platte river. The first joint of the hind tarsi is somewhat less than half the length of the tibia; the antennæ are lost. Differs from the other species by the non-sulcate hind tibiæ.

L. subrufus, rufo-testaceus, nitidus, fronte carinata, thorace latitudine haud breviore, angulis rotundatis, convexo, haud dense punctato, elytris thorace latioribus, ovalibus convexis, subtiliter punctatis, introrsum vix conspicue striatis; tibiis posticis sulcatis, calcare brevi terminatis, antennis corpore vix brevioribus, extrorsum infuscatis. Long. ·12.

Fort Laramie. The upper edge of the hind tibiæ is finely serrate; the tarsus is as long as the tibia.

L. rubidus, apterus, ovatus, piceo-ferrugineus, nitidus, capite infuscato, fronte carinata, vertice transversim impresso, thorace transverso, basi et angulis rotundatis, convexo, alutaceo, subtiliter parce punctulato, elytris ovalibus convexis, sat dense minus subtiliter punctatis, antennis testaceis, extrorsum vix infuscatis, corpore paulo brevioribus. Long. ·11.

Fort Laramie. The spur of the hind tibia is short; the tarsus is as long as the tibia; the elytra are obtusely rounded at tip, and the pygidium is slightly prominent.

GLYPTINA Lec.

G. spuria, testacea, nitida, fronte elevata, vertice bituberculato utrinque oblique impresso, thorace transverso, basi rotundato, lateribus parallelis angulis anticis oblique truncatis, punctato, elytris oblongo-ovalibus thorace latioribus, fortiter punctato-striatis; antennis extrorsum fuscis. Long. ·08.

Fort Laramie. I have given the name *Glyptina* to a group of *Haltica* intermediate between genuine *Haltica* and *Longitarsus*. The head is marked with a deep oblique line each side between the eyes, running forward to the frontal elevation : the antennæ are half as long as the body, slightly thickened externally; the 2d and 3d joints equal in length : the thorax is quadrate, transverse, with the anterior angles obliquely truncate, the disc moderately convex, without impressed lines. The elytra oblong, wider than the thorax, with rows of punctures; the hind tibiæ deeply sulcate above, with the edge of the groove very finely serrate, the terminal spur small, the tarsi attached at the end of the tibiæ, 1st joint equal to the others combined, and nearly half as long as the tibiæ. Besides the two species here described, the Californian *Haltica cerina* Lec., Pacific R. R. Expl. and Surveys, vol. xi, insects, 68, also belongs to this genus.

G. lissotorques, testacea, nitida, fronte parum elevata, vertice utrinque oblique sulcato, thorace transverso, basi rotundato, lateribus parallelis, angulis anticis oblique truncatis, nitido, lævi, vix obsolete parce punctulato, elytris oblongo-ovalibus, thorace latioribus, fortiter punctato-striatis; antennis extrorsum vix infuscatis. Long. ·08.

One specimen with the preceding, which it entirely resembles, except in the sculpture of the head and thorax. It is also found in Pennsylvania.

CHÆTOCNEMA Stephens.

C. subviridis, supra viridi-ænea, obscura, subnitida, thorace latitudine fere duplo breviore, lateribus obliquis late rotundatis, fortius sat dense punctato, elytris fortiter striato-punctatis, interstitiis subtiliter uniseriatim punctulatis, pedibus antennisque nigris, his basi testaceis, tibiis basi vix piceescentibus. Long. ·12.

Fort Laramie. Broader than *C. denticulata*, and differing therefrom in many particulars. I have retained the older name for this genus, as I know no reason for the substitution of Redtenbacher's *Plectroscelis*, which is adopted by many naturalists of Germany and France.

LUPERUS Geoffroy.

L. rufipes, elongatus, chalybeo-niger, thorace parce punctulato, latitudine haud breviore, lateribus late rotundatis subsinuatis, angulis posticis prominulis, elytris fere obsolete punctulatis, chalybeis, antennis pedibusque rufo-testaceis, illis extrorsum fuscis. Long. ·22.

Santa Fé, Messrs. Kern and Fendler. Of the form and size of *L. meraca* (*Galleruca meraca* Say), but known by the uniform color of the feet, the less distinctly punctulate elytra, and the less rounded sides of the thorax.

MICRORHOPALA Chevr.

M. lætula, elongata, postice modice dilatata, et obtuse rotundata, nigra, capite pone antennas, thoraceque toto læte rufo-flavis, hoc parce cribrato, transverso, lateribus obliquis rectis, elytris punctis magnis striatis, seriebus per paria approximatis, internis postice subtilioribus, vittaque utrinque basali ante medium abbreviata flava. Long. ·25.

Fort Riley, Mr. Xantus. Closely related to *M. vittata*, but differs by the sides of the thorax being entirely straight, as well as by the colors; the thorax is very narrowly margined with black, but is yellow both above and beneath, as is also the head, excepting the antennæ, front and mouth, which are black. The outer intervals of the elytra are not shining, and are alternately a little more convex, as in *M. vittata*, and the edge is not serrate.

CASSIDA LINN.

C. ellipsis, elliptica convexa, supra testacea pallida, nitida (quando viva, læte aurea), thorace antice rotundato, margine late explanato hyalino, angulis lateralibus paulo rotundatis, elytris thorace haud latioribus, fortius striato-punctatis, margine subhyalino, antice declivi postice explanato angustius reflexo, capite corporeque nigris, abdomine anguste testaceo marginato, pedibus antennisque flavis, his articulis 3—6 tenuibus æqualibus, 7—11 latioribus, ultimis quatuor nigris. Long. ·26.

One specimen, found near Long's Peak. Allied by the declivous and scarcely explanate but narrowly reflexed elytral margin, to *C. 6-punctata* and *C. 9-maculata*, but differing by the more narrow, regularly elliptical form of body. The legs in *C. 9-maculata* are black; in *C. 6-punctata* they are reddish yellow, but the punctures of the striæ of the elytra in that species are less approximate, each elytron is marked with three black spots, the humeral angles are more prolonged, and the side angles of the thorax are more rounded. Still more essential differences exist in the antennæ: in the present species the 2d joint is a little longer than wide; the 3d is slender, one-half longer than the 2d; the 4th, 5th, and 6th are equal in length and thickness to the 3d; the 7th is more than twice as wide, triangular, pale yellow, like the preceding joints; the remaining four joints are as wide as the 7th, and black. The middle of the anterior margin of the thorax is slightly emarginate, but I suspect this character to be accidental.

C. atripes, ovata, convexa, supra testacea (quando viva læte aurea), thorace antice rotundato, margine hyalino late explanato, angulis externis haud rotundatis, elytris thorace vix latioribus, humeris paulo productis rotundatis, striis e punctis parcis constitutis, margine hyalino antice declivi postice explanato, vix reflexo, utrinque guttis tribus nigris notatis; subtus nigra, abdomine testaceo-marginato, antennis basi flavis, articulis 3—5 æqualibus, 6to paulo latiore, ultimis 5 nigris. Long. ·23.

One specimen, found near Long's Peak. Differs from *C. nigripes* chiefly by the thorax being nearly as wide as the elytra, with the lateral angles scarcely rounded: the margin of the elytra anteriorly is more obliquely declivous than in that species.

With regard to the position of *C. unipunctata* Say, I am somewhat doubtful, although to avoid the multiplication of genera it should probably be allowed to remain in *Cassida*. The 2d joint of the antennæ is scarcely thicker than the 3d, which is about twice as long; the 4th is two-thirds as long as the 3d, and somewhat wider; the 5th is as wide as its length ; and the remaining ones are a little wider than their length: the last is oval and pointed. The ungues, as in our other species, are simple.

BRACHIACANTHA MULS.

B. tau, rotundato-ovalis, convexa, supra rufo-flava, nitida dense subtiliter punctulata, thorace basi subinfuscato, elytris fascia basali ad humerum abbreviata, sutura anguste, guttisque utrinque duabus paulo pone medium nigris, margine externo pone maculas, apicalique nigro, subtus nigra, antennis, palpis, pleuris pedibusque flavis. Long. ·19.

One specimen, Fort Riley: John Xantus, Esq. The head and sides of the thorax are paler than the rest of the upper surface.

EROTYLUS Fabr.

E. **Boisduvalii,** oblongus, ater, subnitidus, elytris sat convexis, albido-testaceis, punctis maioribus nigris minus crebre impressis, singulo macula parva laterali nigra ornato. Loug. ·6—·62. Tab. II, fig. 8.

Chevrolat, Col. Mex. 2d cent. ; Lac. Mon. Erotyl. 466.

A large number of this species was contained in the collection made by Mr. Fendler, near Santa Fé.

INDEX OF GENERA.

LIST OF SPECIES.

I. OF KANSAS AND NEBRASKA.

CICINDELIDÆ.

Amblychila Say.

cylindriformis *Say*.
  A. Piccolominii Reiche.

Megacephala Latr.

virginica *Dej*.
  Cicindela virginica Linn.

Cicindela Linn.

pulchra *Say*.
scutellaris *Say*.
sexguttata *Say*.
purpurea *Oliv*. var. *Audubonii* Lec.
obsoleta *Say*.
prasina *Lec*. Trans. Am. Phil. Soc. XI, 31.
nigrocœrulea *Lec*.
cinctipennis *Lec*.
pusilla *Say*.
cyanella *Lec*. Trans. Am. Phil. Soc. XI, 46.
terricola *Say*.
cuprascens *Lec*.
sperata *Lec*. Trans. Am. Phil. Soc. XI, 50.
lepida *Dej*.
hirticollis *Say*.
  C. albohirta Dej.
vulgaris *Say*.
  C. obliquata Dej.
fulgida *Say*.
venusta *Lec*.
formosa *Say*.
punctulata *Fabr*.
cumatilis *Lec*.
  C. Guexi Chevr.
circumpicta *Fertê*.
  C. Johnsonii Fitch, N. Y. Agr. Soc. 1856, 487.
ecleripes *Lec*.
cursitans *Lec*. Trans. Am. Phil. Soc. XI, 60.
limbata *Say* (fide Say).
decemguttata *Say* (fide Say).

CARABIDÆ.

Brachinus Weber.

cyanipennis *Say*.
and four other species.

Helluomorpha Lap.

laticornis *Lap*.
  Helluo laticornis Dej.
praeusta *Lap*.
  Helluo praeustus Dej.

Galerita Fabr.

dubia *Lec*.
  'Carabus bicolor Drury,' fide Klug.
atripes *Lec*. Proc. Acad. Nat. Sc. 1858, 59.

Lachnophorus Dej.

elegantulus *Mann*.
  Tachypus mediosignatus Ménét.

Casnonia Latr.

pensylvanica *Dej*.
  Attelabus pensylvanicus Linn.

Leptotrachelus Latr.

dorsalis *Latr*.
  Odacantha dorsalis Fabr.
  Sphæracra dorsalis Say.

Lebia Latr.

viridipennis *Dej*.
  L. borea Hentz.
smaragdula *Dej*.
viridis *Say; Dej*.
pumila *Dej*.
  L. floricola Harris.
solea *Hentz*.
  L. scapularis Dej.
furcata *Lec*.
axillaris *Dej*.

Blechrus Motsch.

linearis *Schaum.* Ins. Deutschl. I, 275.
Dromius angustus‖Lec.
Bomius linearis Lec.

Axinopalpus Lec.

biplagiatus *Lec.*
Dromius biplagiatus Dej.

Glycia Chaud.

viridicollis *Lec.*
Cymindis viridicollis Lec.
purpurea *Lec.*
Cymindis purpurea Say.
var. *Cymindis amoena* Lec.

Calleida Dej.

punctata *Lec.*
smaragdina *Dej.*

Cymindis Latr.

laticollis *Say.*
cribricollis *Dej.*
cribrata *Lec.*
pilosa *Say*
C. pubescens Dej.

Calathus Bon.

gregarius *Dej.*
Feronia gregaria Say.

Rhadine Lec.

larvalis *Lec.*

Platynus Bon. emend. Brullé.

extensicollis *Lec.* Proc. Acad. Nat. Sc. VII, 46.
Feronia extensicollis Say.
Feronia (Anchomenus) proximus Harris.
Anchomenus extensicollis Dej.
Anchomenus obscuratus Chaud.
Anchomenus Lecontei Lec.
Anchomenus elongatulus‡Lec.
Anchomenus viridis Lec.
punctiformis *Lec.* ibid. VII, 50.
Feronia punctiformis Say.
Agonum rufipes Dej.
Agonum foveicolle Chaud.
errans *Lec.* ibid. VII, 50.
Feronia errans Say.
subcordatus *Lec.* ibid. VII, 51.
Agonum erythropum‖Kirby.
basalis *Lec.* Proc. Acad. Nat. Sc. VII, 52.
Agonum basale Lec.

nutans *Lec.* ibid. VII, 52.
Feronia nutans Say.
Agonum femoratum Dej.
picipennis *Lec.* ibid. VII, 53.
Agonum picipenne Kirby.
chalceus *Lec.* Agassiz' Lake Sup. 205.
Agonum chalceum Lec.
maculifrons *Say* (Feronia), (fide Say).
scutellaris *Say* (Feronia), (fide Say).
? *Agonum melanarium* Dej.
? *Platynus melanarius* Lec.

Evarthrus Lec.

sigillatus *Lec.* Journ. Acad. Nat. Sc. 2d ser. II, 228.
Feronia sigillata Say.
Feronia vidua Dej.
seximpressus *Lec.* ibid.
Feronia seximpressa Lec.
corax *Lec.* ibid. II, 229.
Feronia corax Lec.
abdominalis *Lec.* ibid. II, 232.
Feronia abdominalis Lec.
lixa *Lec.* ibid.
Feronia lixa Lec.
incisus *Lec.* ibid.
Feronia incisa Lec.
ovipennis *Lec.* ibid.
Feronia ovipennis Lec.
latebrosus *Lec.* ibid. II, 233.
constrictus *Lec.* ibid.
Feronia constricta Say
substriatus *Lec.* ibid.
Feronia substriata Say.
colossus *Lec.* ibid.
Feronia colossus Say.
heros *Hald.* Proc. Acad. Nat. Sc. VI, 361.
Feronia heros Say.

Pterostichus Bon.

caudicalis *Lec.*
Feronia caudicalis! Say.
Feronia luctuosa Dej.
Omaseus nigrita‡Kirby.
Pterostichus luctuosus Lec. loc. cit. II, 243.
mutus *Lec.*
Feronia muta Say.
Feronia morosa Dej.
Omaseus picicornis Kirby.

Poecilus Bon.

scitulus *Lec.*
cyaneus *Lec.*
chalcites ——.
Feronia chalcites Say.
Poecilus Sayi Brullé.

lucublandus *Kirby*.
  Feronia lucublanda Say.
bicolor *Lec.*

Amara Bon.
laticollis *Lec.*
  ? Curtonotus convexiusculus‡Kirby.
carinata *Lec.*
furtiva *Say.*
libera *Lec.* Proc. Acad. Nat. Sc. VII, 349.
Isopleurus hyperboreus‡Lec.
  ? Curtonotus latior Kirby.
angustata *Say.*
  A. indistincta Hald.
impuncticollis *Say.*
  A. difficilis Lec.
subpunctata *Lec.* Proc. Acad. Nat. Sc. VII, 352.
confusa *Lec.*
polita *Lec.*
obesa *Say.*
  A. patricia‡Dej.
  Feronia obesa Say.
diffinis *Lec.* Proc. Acad. Nat. Sc. VII, 354.
  Percosia diffinis Lec.
terrestris *Lec.* Proc. Acad. Nat. Sc. VII, 354.
  Isopleurus terrestris Lec.
musculus *Say.*
  Acrodon musculis et *contempta* Lec.

Nothopus Lec.
zabroides *Lec.*
  Euryderus‖*zabroides* Lec.

Geopinus Lec.
incrassatus *Lec.*
  Daptus incrassatus Dej.

Cratognathus Dej.
setosus *Lec.* Trans. Am. Phil. Soc. X, 381.
  Piosoma setosum Lec.

Cratacanthus Dej.
dubius *Lec.*
  Harpalus dubius Beauv.
  Cratacanthus pensylvanicus Dej.

Agonoderus Dej.
lineola *Dej.*
  Carabus lineola Fabr.
dorsalis *Lec.*
pallipes *Dej.*
  Carabus pallipes Fabr.

Discoderus Lec.
parallelus *Lec.* Trans. Am. Phil. Soc. X, 382.
  Selenophorus parallelus Hald.
5

tenebrosus *Lec.* ibid. 382.
  Selenophorus tenebrosus Lec.

Spongopus Lec.
verticalis *Lec.*

Anisodactylus Dej.
rusticus *Dej.*
  Harpalus rusticus Say.
  Anisodactylus pinguis Lec.
  Anisodactylus gravidus Lec.
  Anisodactylus crassus Lec.
agricola *Dej.*
  Harpalus agricolus Say.
  Harpalus paradoxus Hald.
  Anisodactylus striatus Lec.
baltimorensis *Dej.*
  Harpalus baltimorensis Say.
cænus *Dej.*
  Harpalus cænus Say.

Eurytrichus Lec.
terminatus *Lec.*
  Feronia terminata Say.
  Harpalus terminatus Dej.

Harpalus Latr.
impotens *Lec.* Journ. Acad. Nat. Sc. 2d ser. IV, 11.
pedicularius *Lec.*
  Selenophorus pedicularius Dej.
troglodytes *Lec.*
  Selenophorus troglodytes Dej.
æreus *Lec.*
  Selenophorus æreus Lec.
  Selenophorus planipennis Lec.
ellipticus *Lec.*
  Selenophorus ellipticus Dej.
caliginosus *Say.*
  Carabus caliginosus Fabr.
amputatus *Say.*
  H. Stephensii Kirby.
rotundicollis *Kirby.*
pensylvanicus *Lec.*
  Carabus pensylvanicus De Geer.
  Carabus bicolor Fabr.
  Harpalus faunus‡Dej.
compar *Lec.*
  H. pensylvanicus Say.
  H. bicolor‡Dej.
stupidus *Lec.*, ante, 3.
oblitus *Lec.*, ante, 2.
nitidulus *Chaud.*
herbivagus *Say.*
ellipsis *Lec.*
ventralis *Lec.*
funestus *Lec.*

Stenolophus Dej.
ochropezus *Dej.*
Feronia ochropeza Say.
humilis *Lec.*
Acupalpus humilis Dej.
dissimilis *Dej.*

Bradycellus Er.
obesulus *Lec.*
badiipennis *Lec.*
Geobænus ruficrus‡Lec.
Stenolophus badiipennis Hald.
congener *Lec.*
Geobænus congener Lec.
rupestris *Lec.*
Trechus rupestris Say.
Acupalpus elongatulus Dej.
Trechus flavipes Kirby.

Badister Clairv.
notatus *Hald.*
B. terminalis Lec.
micans *Lec.*

Diplochila Brullé.
laticollis *Lec.*
gens maior Lec.
obtusa *Lec.*

Dicælus Bon
lævigatus *Lec.*
splendidus *Say.*
sculptilis *Say.*
simplex *Dej.*
 var. *D. obscurus* Lec.
elongatus *Dej.*

Oodes Bon.
amaroides *Dej.*

Atranus Lec.
pubescens *Lec.*
Anchomenus pubescens Dej.
Anchomenus obconicus Hald.

Chlænius Bon.
purpuricollis *Randall.*
tomentosus *Dej.*
Eponis tomentosus Say.
Amara luctuosa Germ.
pensylvanicus *Say.*
C. vicinus Dej.
C. pubescens Harris.
vafer *Lec.* Proc. Acad. Nat. Sc. VI, 66.

æstivus *Say.*
C. cobaltinus Dej.
erythropus Germ.
C. rufilabris Dej.
laticollis *Say.*
C. diffinis Chaud. Bull. Mosc. 1856, II, 279. *
lithophilus *Say.*
C. viridanus Dej.
sericeus *Say.*
Carabus sericeus Forster.
Chlænius perviridis Lec.
solitarius *Say.*
brevilabris *Lec.*
 var. C. consimilis Lec.
impunctifrons *Say.*
C. emarginatus‡Kirby.

Anomoglossa Chaud.
emarginata *Chaud.* Bull. Mosc.
Chlænius emarginatus Dej.

Pasimachus Bon.
validus *Lec.*
P. punctulatus‡Lec.
elongatus *Lec.*
obsoletus *Lec.*
costifer *Lec.* Proc. Acad. Nat. Sc. VII, 79.

Scarites Fabr.
subterraneus *Fabr.* cum var.

Clivina Latr.
bipustulata *Dej.*
Scarites bipustulatus Fabr.
Scarites quadrimaculatus Beauv.
postica *Lec.*

Aspidoglossa Putz.
subangulata *Lec.*
Clivina crenata‡Dej.
Dyschirius subangulatus Chaud.
Dyschirius humeralis Chaud.
Aspidoglossa fraterna Putz.
Aspidoglossa vicina Putz.
Clivina bipustulata‡Say.

Dyschirius Bon.
sulcatus *Lec.*
apicalis‖Lec.
sphæricollis *Putz.*
Clivina sphæricollis Say.

Tachys Knoch.
vivax *Lec.*
 var. T. mendax Lec.

incurvus *Lec.*
    Bembidium incurrum Say.
    var. *Tachys anceps* Lec.
pulchellus *Ferté.*
dolosus *Lec.*
sequax *Lec.*
corruscus *Lec.*
inornatus *Lec.*
    Bembidium inornatum Say.
    Tachyta picipes Kirby.
flavicauda *Lec.*
    Bembidium flavicaudum Say.

Bembidium Latr. (emend. Lec.)

punctato-striatum *Say.*
stigmaticum Dej.
? *sigillare* Say.
inæquale *Say.*
    arenarium Dej.
lævigatum *Say.*
    Hydrium lævigatum Lec.
coxendix *Say.*
    Odontium coxendix Lec.
americanus *Dej.*
cordatum *Lec.*
dorsale *Say.*
umbratum *Lec.*
viridicolle *Lec.*
    Notaphus viridicollis Ferté.
patruele *Dej.*
rapidum *Lec.*
timidum *Lec.*
pictum *Lec.*
quadrimaculatum *Gyll.*
    Carabus quadrimaculatus Linn.
    Bembidium oppositum Say.
affine *Say, Dej.*
    Bembidium fallax Dej.
bimaculatum *Lec.*
    Peryphus bimaculatus Kirby.
perspicuum *Lec.*
cautum *Lec.*
nitidum *Lec.*
    Eudromus nitidus Kirby.

Cychrus Fabr.

elevatus *Fabr.*
heros *Harris.*

Nomaretus Lec.

cavicollis *Lec.*, ante, 3.

Carabus Linn.

serratus *Say.*
    C. lineatopunctatus Dej.

Calosoma Fabr.

luxatum *Say.*
striatulum *Lec.*, ante, 4.
scrutator *Fabr.*
calidum *Fabr.*
    var.? *C. lepidum* Lec.
obsoletum *Say.*
    C. luxatum‡Dej.
triste *Lec.*
externum *Lec.*
    Carabus externus Say.
    Calosoma longipenne Dej.

Elaphrus Fabr.

Clairvillei *Kirby.*
intermedius *Kirby.*
californicus *Mann.*
    var.? *E. similis* Lec.

Omophron Latr.

americanum *Dej.*
    O. Sayi Kirby.
nitidum *Lec.*

DYTISCIDÆ.

Haliplus Latr.

fasciatus *Aubé.*
immaculicollis *Harris.*
    H. americanus Aubé.
    H. impressus‡Kirby, teste White, Brit. Mus.
    Cat. 3.

Hydroporus Clairv.

punctatus *Aubé.*
    Laccophilus punctatus Say.
cuspidatus *Germ.*
    Hyphidrus notatus Say.
lacustris *Say.*
    H. pulicarius Aubé.
mixtus *Lec.* Proc. Acad. Nat. Sc. VII, 296.
semirufus *Lec.* ibid.
vittatus *Lec.* ibid.
catascopium *Say.*
    H. interruptus Say.
    H. parallelus Say.
concinnus *Lec.* Proc. Acad. Nat. Sc. VII, 297.
patruelis *Lec.* ibid. VII, 298.
nubilus *Lec.* ibid. VII, 298.
discoideus *Lec.* ibid. VII, 299.

Laccophilus Leach.

maculosus *Say.*
americanus *Aubé.*

Coptotomus Say.

longulus *Lec.*

Copelatus Er.

glyphicus *Lec.*
  Colymbetes glyphicus Say.
  Copelatus 10-*striatus* Aubé.

Agabus Leach.

clavatus *Lec.*, ante, 4.
griscipennis *Lec.*, ante, 5.
obliteratus *Lec.*, ante, 5.
spilotus *Lec.*, ante, 5.
tæniolatus *Lec.*
  Colymbetes tæniolatus Harris.
  Agabus tæniatus Aubé.

Ilybius Er.

laramæus *Lec.*, ante, 4.

Colymbetes Clairv.

binotatus *Harris.*
  C. maculicollis Aubé.

Acilius Leach.

ornaticollis *Aubé.*
  Thermonectes irroratus Mels.

Eunectes Er.

sticticus *Er.*
  Dytiscus sticticus Linn.

Cybister Curtis.

fimbriolatus *Lec.*
  Dytiscus fimbriolatus Say.
  Cybister dissimilis Aubé.

Dytiscus Linn.

anxius *Mann.*
  D. marginicollis Lec.
Harrisii *Kirby.*

GYRINIDÆ.

Dineutes M'Leay.

two species.

HYDROPHILIDÆ.

Helophorus Fabr.

linearis *Lec.* Proc. Acad. Nat. Sc. VII, 357.
lineatus *Say.*

Laccobius Er.

agilis *Lec.* Proc. Acad. Nat. Sc. VII, 363.
  Hydrophilus agilis Randall.
  Laccobius punctulatus Mels.

Berosus Leach.

fraternus *Lec.* Proc. Acad. Nat. Sc. VII, 364.

Hydrophilus Geoffr.

triangularis *Say.*
  Hydrophilus lugubris Motsch.
  Stethoxus subsulcatus Lec. Proc. Acad. Nat.
    Sc. VII, 221.
lateralis Fabr.
  H. niubatus Say.
sublævis *Lec.* Proc. Acad. Nat. Sc. VII, 368.
glaber *Herbst.*

Philhydrus Solier.

nebulosus *Lec.*
  Hydrophilus nebulosus Say.
diffusus *Lec.* Proc. Acad. Nat. Sc. VII, 371.
perplexus *Lec.* ibid.
cinctus *Lec.*
  Hydrophilus cinctus Say.
  Philhydrus limbatis Mels.

Hydrobius Leach.

subcupreus *Lec.*
  Hydrophilus subcupreus Say.

STAPHYLINIDÆ.[1]

Falagria Mann.

venustula *Er.*

Xantholinus Dahl.

obscurus *Er.*

Staphylinus Linn.

villosus *Grav.*
cinnamopterus *Grav.*

[1] Besides the described species of this family mentioned above, nondescripts of the following genera are contained in my collection, but the description of them at present would be attended with no advantage to science, on account of the multitude of other species that remain unknown: they must therefore await the monographing of the entire group.

Myrmedonia, Homalota, Tachyusa, Conurus, Tachinus, Boletobius, Philonthus, Acylophorus, Quedius, Lathrobium, Stenus, Bledius, Oxytelus, Trogophlœus, Apocellus, Boreaphilus, Omalium.

Philonthus Leach.
hepaticus *Er.*

Acylophorus Nordm.
flavicollis *Sachse.*

Sunius Leach.
longiusculus *Er.*
   Pæderus longiusculus Mann.
   Pæderus discopunctatus Say.
? binotatus *Say* (Pæderus), (fide Say)

Pæderus Fabr.
littorarius *Grav.*

Lithocharis Er.
confluens *Er.*
   Lathrobium confluentum Say.

Stenus Latr.
egenus *Er.*
flavicornis *Er.*
punctatus *Er.*

Euæsthetus Grav.
americanus *Er.*

Bledius Leach.
pallipennis *Er.* (fide Say).
   Oxytelus pallipennis Say.
armatus *Er.* (fide Say).
   Oxytelus armatus Say.
melanocephalus *Er.* (fide Say).
   Oxytelus melanocephalus Say.
fasciatus *Er.* (fide Say).
   Oxytelus fasciatus Say.

Osorius Leach.
latipes *Er.*

Anthophagus Grav.
brunneus *Say.*

Glyptoma Er.
costale *Er.*

PSELAPHIDÆ.

Tyrus Aubé.
humeralis *Lec.*
   Hamotus humeralis Aubé, teste Schaum.
   Tyrus compar Lec.

Bryaxis Leach.
rubicunda *Aubé.*

SILPHIDÆ.

Necrophorus Fabr.
mediatus *Fabr.*
marginatus *Fabr.*
Melsheimeri *Kirby.*
pustulatus *Herschel.*
   N. bicolon Newman.
orbicollis *Say.*
   N. Hallii Kirby.
velutinus *Fabr.*
   N. tomentosus Weber.

Silpha Linn.
surinamensis *Fabr.*
lapponica *Herbst.*
   Silpha caudata Say.
   Silpha tuberculata Germ.
   Silpha californica Mann.
   Oiceoptoma granigera Chevr.
truncata *Say.*
peltata *Lec.* Proc. Acad. Nat. Sc. VI, 279.
   Scarabæus peltatus Catesby.
   Silpha americana Linn.
ramosa *Say.*
bituberosa *Lec.*, ante, 6.

Catops Fabr.
simplex *Say* (fide Say).
basillaris *Say* (fide Say).

Agathidium Illiger.
exiguum *Mels.*
   A. ruficorne Lec.
? pallidum *Say* (fide Say).

PHALACRIDÆ.

Phalacrus Payk.
penicillatus *Say.*
seriatus *Lec.* Proc. Acad. Nat. Sc. VIII, 15.
simplex *Lec.* ibid.

Olibrus Er.
pallipes *Lec.* Proc. Acad. Nat. Sc. VIII, 17.
   Phalacrus pallipes Say.
striatulus *Lec.* Proc. Acad. Nat. Sc. VIII, 16.
semistriatus *Lec.* ibid.

NITIDULIDÆ.

Carpophilus Leach.
caudalis *Lec.* Proc. Acad. Nat. Sc. 1859, 70.
apicalis *Lec.* ante, 6.

carbonatus *Lec.*, ante, 6.
pallipennis *Lec.*
  Cercus pallipennis Say.
  Carpophilus floralis Er.

Epuræa Er.
rufa *Er.*
  Nitidula rufa Say.

Nitidula Fabr. (emend. Er.)
ziezae *Say.*
uniguttata *Mels.*

Omosita Er.
colon *Er.*
  Nitidula colon Fabr.

Phenolia Er.
grossa *Er.*
  Nitidula grossa Fabr.

Meligethes Steph.
ruficornis *Lec.*, ante, 6.
sævus *Lec.*, ante, 6.

Pocadius Er.
helvolus *Er.*

Pallodes Er.
silaceus *Er.*

Cryptarcha Er.
strigata *Er.*
  Nitidula strigata Fabr.

Ips Fabr.
sanguinolentus *Oliv.*
quadrisignatus *Say.*
bipunctatus *Say.*
  Colydium bipunctatum Say.

Trogosita Oliv.
castanea *Mels.*
corticalis *Mels.*

LATHRIDIIDÆ.

Lathridius Herbst.
? 8-dentatus *Say* (fide Say).
  ? *Corticaria denticulata* Kirby.

COLYDIIDÆ.

Bothrideres Er.
geminatus *Er.* (nec *Hald.*)
  Lyctus geminatus Say.

Cerylon Latr.
castaneum *Say.*
unicolor *Lec.*
  Lathridius unicolor Ziegler.

CUCUJIDÆ.

Læmophlœus Er.
biguttatus *Mels.*
  Cucujus biguttatus Say.
  Læmophlœus bisignatus Guér.

Brontes Fabr.
dubius *Fabr.*

Silvanus Latr.
planatus *Germ.*
dentatus *Say.*
  Lyctus dentatus Fabr.

DERMESTIDÆ.

Dermestes Linn.
marmoratus *Say.*
nubilus *Say.*
caninus *Germ.*
elongatus *Lec.*
vulpinus *Fabr.*

HETEROCERIDÆ.

Heterocerus Fabr.
pallidus *Say* (fide Say).
pusillus *Say* (fide Say).

GEORYSSIDÆ.

Georyssus Latr.
pusillus *Lec.* Proc. Acad. Nat. Sc. VI, 44.

SCAPHIDIIDÆ.

Scaphidium Oliv.
4-pustulatum *Say.*

HISTERIDÆ.

Hololepta Payk.
fossularis *Say.*
  æqualis *Say* (fem.)
lucida *Lec.*

Hister Linn.

instratus *Lec.*, ante, 7.
biplagiatus *Lec.*
dispar *Lec.*
depurator *Say.*
abbreviatus Fabr.
nubilus *Lec.*, ante, 7.
pollutus *Lec.*, ante, 7.
americanus *Payk.*
subrotundus *Er.*
carolinus *Payk.*
Lecontei *Lec.*
  Platysoma depressum‡Er., Lec.
  Platysoma Lecontei Marscul.
parallelus *Say.*

Paromalus Er.
æqualis *Er.*
  Hister æqualis Say.
bistriatus *Er.*

aprinus Leach.
lugens *Er.*
  californicus Mann.
spurcus *Lec.*, ante, 7.
parumpunctatus *Lec.*, ante, 7.
pratensis *Lec.*, ante, 8.
pensylvanicus *Er.*
  Hister pensylvanicus Payk.
patruelis *Lec.*

Plegaderus Leach.
transversus *Lec.*
  Hister transversus Say.

Acritus Lec.
exiguus *Lec.*
  Abræus exiguus Er.

SCARABÆIDÆ.

Xyloryctes Hope.
satyrus *Burm.*
  Geotrupes satyrus Fabr.

Phileurus Latr.
valgus *Dej.*
  Geotrupes valgus Fabr.
  Phileurus castaneus Hald.

Strategus Hope.
mormon *Burm.*

Aphonus Lec.
pyriformis *Lec.* Proc. Acad. Nat. Sc. VIII, 21.
  Bothynus pyriformis Lec.

tridentatus *Lec.* ibid. VIII, 22.
  Scarabæus tridentatus Say.
  Bothynus tridentatus Lec.

Ligyrus Burm.
gibbosus *Lec.* Proc. Acad. Nat. Sc. VIII, 20.
  Scarabæus gibbosus DeGeer.
  Podalgus variolosus Burm.
relictus *Lec.* Proc. Acad. Nat. Sc. VIII, 21.
  Scarabæus relictus Say.
  Heteronychus relictus Burm.

Osmoderma Lepell.
eremicola *Gory.*
  Cetonia eremicola Knoch.

Cremastochilus Knoch.
nitens *Lec.* Proc. Acad. Nat. Sc. VI, 232.
Knochii *Lec.* ibid. VI, 231.
saucius *Lec.* Journ. Acad. Nat. Sc. 2d ser. IV, 16.

Euryomia Burm. (emend. Lac.)
inda Lac. Gen. Col. III, 528.
  Scarabæus indus Linn.
  Cetonia barbata Say.
  Erirhipis inda Burm.
melancholica *Lac.* Gen. Col. III, 527.
  Cetonia melancholica Gory.
  Euphoria melancholica Schaum.
sepulchralis *Lac.* ibid.
  Cetonia sepulchralis Fabr.
  Cetonia Reichii Gory.
  Euphoria sepulchralis Burm.
fulgida *Lac.* Gen. Col. III, 528.
  Cetonia fulgida Fabr.
  Erirhipis fulgida Fabr.
areata *Lac.* Gen. Col. III, 528.
  Cetonia areata Fabr.
  Stephanucha areata Burm.

Allorhina Burm. (emend. Lac.)
nitida *Lac.* Gen. Col. III, 497.
  Scarabæus nitidus Linn.
  Cotinis nitida Burm.

Anomala Samouelle (emend. Burm.).
minuta *Burm.*
marginata *Burm.*
  Melolontha marginata Fabr.
  Melolontha annulata Germ.
varians *Burm.*
  Melolontha varians Fabr.

Strigoderma Burm.

arboricola Burm.
　Melolontha arboricola Fabr.

Polyphylla Harris.

decemlineata *Lec.* (infra).
　Melolontha 10-*lineata* Say.
Hammondi *Lec.* J. Ac. Nat. Sc. 2d ser. III, 228.

Lachnosterna Hope.

lanceolata *Lec.* J. Ac. Nat. Sc. 2d ser. III, 237.
　Melolontha lanceolata Say.
　Tostegoptera lanceolata Blanchard.
frontalis *Lec.* J. Ac. Nat. Sc. 2d ser. III, 239.
longitarsis *Lec.* ibid.
　Melolontha longitarsis Say.
futilis *Lec.*
fusca *Lec.* Journ. Acad. Sc. 2d ser. III, 244.
　Melolontha fusca Fröhl.
　Melolontha quercina Knoch.
　Melolontha fervens Gyll.
　Melolontha fervida‡Oliv.
cephalica *Lec.* J. Ac. Nat. Sc. 2d ser. III, 245.
fraterna *Lec.* ibid. III, 249.
　Phyllophaga fraterna Harris.
　Ancylonycha fraterna Blanch.
rugosa *Lec.* ibid. III, 252.
　Ancylonycha rugosa Mels.
affinis *Lec.* ibid. III, 252.
ciliata *Lec.* ibid. III, 253.
hirticula *Hope.*
　Melolontha hirticula Knoch.
　Melolontha hirsuta‡Say.
robusta *Lec.* ibid. III, 257.
crenulata *Lec.* ibid. III, 258.
　Melolontha crenulata Fröhl.
　Melolontha georgicana Gyll.
　Phyllophaga georgicana Harris.
　Ancylonycha crenulata Blanch.
glabricula *Lec.* ibid. III, 260.
tristis *Lec.* ibid. III, 261.
　Melolontha tristis Fabr.
　Melolontha pilosicollis Knoch.
　Trichesthes pilosicollis Er.
　Trichestes tristis Burm.

Listrochelus Blanch.

obtusus *Lec.* Journ. Acad. Nat. Sc. 2d ser. III, 264.
falsus *Lec.* ibid.
fimbripes *Lec.* ibid.

Diplotaxis Kirby.

obscura *Lec.*, ante, 9.
Harperi *Blanch.*

frondicola *Lec.*
　Melolontha frondicola Say.
　Diplotaxis testacea Burm.
truncatula *Lec.* J. Ac. Nat. Sc. 2d ser. III, 269.
morula *Lec.* ibid. III, 270.
Haydenii *Lec.* ibid. III, 272.
innoxia *Lec.* ibid. III, 273.

Diazus Lec.

rudis *Lec.*, ante, 10.

Dichelonycha Kirby.

truncata *Lec.* J. Ac. Nat. Sc. 2d ser. III, 281.

Serica M'Lcay.

vespertina *Dej.*
　Melolontha vespertina Gyll. Say.
　Camptorhina atricapilla Kirby.
sericea Burm.
　Melolontha sericea Say.
curvata *Lec.* J. Ac. Nat. Sc. 2d ser. III, 276.

Macrodactylus Latr.

angustatus *Lec.* J. Ac. Nat. Sc. 2d ser. III, 278.
　Melolontha elongata||Herbst.
　Melolontha angustata Beauv.
　Macrodactylus polyphagus Burm.

Hoplia Illiger.

laticollis *Lec.* J. Ac. Nat. Sc. 2d ser. III, 284.

Geotrupes Latr.

opacus *Hald.* Proc. Acad. Nat. Sc. 2d ser. VI, 362.

Odontæus Klug.

filicornis *Say.*
　Geotrupes filicornis Say.

Bolbocerus Kirby.

lazarus *Klug.*
　Geotrupes lazarus Fabr.
　Geotrupes melibœus Fabr.

Canthon Hoffmans.

lœvis *Mels.*
　Scarabæus pilularius||De Geer.
　Scarabæus lævis Drury.
　Ateuchus volvens Fabr.
chalcites *Mels.*
　Coprobius chalcites Hald.
ebenus *Mels.*
　Ateuchus ebenus Say.
nigricornis *Mels.*
　Ateuchus nigricornis Say.
praticola *Lec.*, ante, 10.

viridis *Mels.*
  Ateuchus viridis Beauv.
  Onthophagus viridicatus Say.
  Ateuchus obsoletus Say.

Onthophagus Latr.

orpheus.
  Scarabæus orpheus Panzer.
  Copris canadensis Fabr.
Hecate.
  Scarabæus Hecate Panzer.
  Copris latebrosus Fabr.
  Copris hastator Fabr.
  Copris oblectus Beauv.

Phanæus M'Leay.

carnifex *M'Leay.*
  Scarabæus carnifex Linn.
triangularis *Lec.*
  Copris triangularis Say.
  Phanæus torrens Lec.

Copris Geoffr.

anaglypticus *Say.*
ammon *Fabr.*

Ochodæus Latr.

• musculus *Lec.*
  Bolbocerus musculus Say.
  Ochodæus americanus Westwood.

Aphodius Illiger.

denticulatus *Hald.*
curtus *Hald.*
granarius *Illiger.*
  Scarabæus granarius Linn.
  Aphodius 4-tuberculatus Fabr.
vittatus *Say.*
femoralis *Say.*
concavus *Say.*
  A. lævigatus Hald.
oblongus *Say.*
  A. badipes Mels.

Euparia Lep. (emend. Er.)

stercorator *Er.*
  Aphodius stercorator Fabr.
strigata *Lec.*
  Aphodius strigatus Say.

Trox Fabr.

alternans *Lec.* Proc. Acad. Nat. Sc. VII, 211.
tuberculatus *Ol.*
  Scarabæus tuberculatus DeG.

  Trox canaliculatus Say.
  Trox serrulatus Beauv.
sordidus *Lec.* ibid VII, 211.
capillaris *Say.*
atrox *Lec.* Proc. Acad. Nat. Sc. VII, 214.

Omorgus Er.

scutellaris *Lec.* Proc. Acad. Nat. Sc. VII, 214.
  Trox scutellaris Say.
pustulatus *Lec.*
  Trox tuberculatus‡Beauv.
punctatus *Lec.* Proc. Acad. Nat. Sc. VII, 215.
  Trox punctatus Germ.
  Trox alternatus Say.
erinaceus *Lec.*
morsus *Lec.* ibid. VII, 216.

Lucanus Linn.

capreolus *Linn.*
  L. dama Thunberg.
placidus *Say.*
  L. lentus Lap. Hist. Nat. II, 171.

Dorcus M'Leay.

parallelus *Burm.*
  Lucanus parallelus Say.

Platycerus Geoffr.

quercus *Schönh.*
  Lucanus quercus Weber.
  Platycerus securidens Say.

BUPRESTIDÆ.

Ancylochira Esch.

confluens *Lec.*
  Buprestis confluenta Say.
maculiventris *Lec.*
  Buprestis maculiventris Say.
  Buprestis sexnotata Lap.
  Anoplis rusticorum Kirby.

Chalcophora Sol.

campestris *Lec.* (fide Say).
  Buprestis campestris Say.
  Buprestis substrigosa Lap. & Gory.

Melanophila Esch.

longipes *Lec.*
  Apatura appendiculata‡Lap. & Gory.
  Bup. (Oxypteris) appendiculata‡Kirby.
  Melanophila immaculata Gory.
atropurpurea *Lec.*
  Buprestis atropurpurea Say.

6

fulvoguttata *Lec.*
  Buprestis fulvoguttata Harris.
  Apatura octospilota Lap. & Gory.
  Apatura croceosignata Lap. & Gory.
  Apatura decolorata Lap. & Gory.

Anthaxia Esch.
quercata *Dej.*
  Buprestis quercata Fabr.
viridicornis *Dej.*
  Buprestis viridicornis Say.

Chrysobothris Esch.
sexguttata *Lec.*
  Buprestis sexguttata Say.

Psiloptera Sol.
Woodhousei *Lec.*
  Dicerca? *Woodhousei* Lec. Proc. Acad. Nat.
    Sc. VI, 68.
  var. *P. valens* Lec. ibid. 1858, 66.

Dicerca Esch.
prolongata *Lec.*

Poecilonota Esch.
cyanipes *Lec.*
  Buprestis cyanipes Say.

Acmæodera Esch.
mixta *Lec.* Trans. Am. Phil. Soc. XI, 227.

Ptosima Serv.
gibbicollis *Lec.*
  Buprestis gibbicollis Say.
  Ptosima luctuosa Gory.

Agrilus Lap.
bilineatus *Say.*
  Buprestis bilineata Weber.
  Agrilus bivittatus Kirby.
  Agrilus flavolineatus Mann.
  Agrilus aurolineatus Gory.
latebrus *Lap.*
granulatus *Say.*
politus *Say.*
defectus *Lec.* Trans. Am. Phil. Soc. XI, 244.
pusillus *Say.*
obolinus *Lec.* Trans. Am. Phil. Soc. XI, 248.
otiosus *Say.*
lateralis *Say.*

Brachys Sol.
terminans *Lap.*
  Buprestis terminans Fabr.

ELATERIDÆ.

Tharops Lap.
ruficornis *Lec.* Trans. Am. Phil. Soc. X, 411.
  Melasis ruficornis Say.

Hylochares Latr.
nigricornis *Lec.* Trans. Am. Phil. Soc. X, 413.
  Melasis nigricornis Say.

Microrhagus Esch.
triangularis *Lec.* Trans. Am. Phil. Soc. X, 419.
  Elater triangularis Say.

Pedetes Kirby.
cucullatus *Lec.* Trans. Am. Phil. Soc. X, 425.
  Elater cucullatus Say.
  Athous hypoleucus Mels.
  Athous procericollis Mels.
  Athous strigatus Mels.

Limonius Esch.
auripilis *Lec.* Trans. Am. Phil. Soc. X, 429.
  Elater auripilis Say.
quercinus *Dej.*
  Elater quercinus Say.
basillaris *Lec.* Trans. Am. Phil. Soc. X, 431.
  Elater basillaris Say.

Cratonychus Er.
macer *Lec.* Trans. Am. Phil. Soc. X, 473.
incertus *Lec.* Trans. Am. Phil. Soc. X, 474.
clandestinus *Er.*
fissilis *Lec.*
  Cratonychus laticollis Er.
  ?Elater brevicollis Herbst.
  Elater cinereus (fissilis) Say.
  Elater (Melanotus) cinereus Harris.
  Cratonychus ochraceipennis Mels.
  Cratonychus sphenoïdalis Mels.
communis *Er.*
  Elater communis Gyll.
  Elater cinereus Weber.
cribulosus *Lec.* Trans. Am. Phil. Soc. X, 478.

Monocrepidius Esch.
vespertinus *Dej.*
  Elater vespertinus Fabr.
  Elater finitimus Say.
  Monocrepidius serotinus Germ.
auritus *Germ.*
  Elater auritus Herbst.
  Oophorus crassicollis Mels
bellus *Dej.*
  Elater bellus Say.
  Cryptohypnus bellus Germ.

Æolus Esch.
dorsalis *Candèze*, Mon. Elat. II, 285.
  Elater dorsalis Say.
  Cryptohypnus dorsalis Germ.

Œdostethus Lec.
femoralis *Lec.* Trans. Am. Phil. Soc. X, 489.

Adelocera Latr.
impressicollis *Lec.* Trans. Am. Phil. Soc. X, 490.
  Elater impressicollis Say.
  Elater lepturus Say.
  Adelocera senilis Germ.
marmorata *Germ.*
  Elater marmoratus Fabr.

Lacon Lap.
rectangularis *Candèze*, Mon. El. I, 155.
  Elater rectangularis Say.

Melanactes Lec.
piceus *Lec.* Trans. Am. Phil. Soc. X, 494.
  Elater piceus DeGeer.
  Elater lævigatus Fabr.
  Elater morio (var.) Say.
  Pristilophus lævigatus Germ.
  Pristilophus femoralis Mels.
puncticollis *Lec.* Trans. Am. Phil. Soc. X, 495.
  Pristilophus puncticollis Lec. Proc. Ac. Nat.
    Sc. VI, 68.

Alaus Esch.
oculatus *Esch.*
  Elater oculatus Fabr.
myops *Esch.*
  Elater myops Fabr.
  Elater luscus‡Oliv.
gorgops *Lec.* Journ. Acad. Nat. Sc. 2d ser. IV, 35.
  Alaus oculatus (var.) Lec. Trans. Am. Phil.
    Soc. 10, 496.

Cardiophorus Esch.
erythropus *Er.*
  Cardiophorus amictus Mels.
  ?Elater convexus Say.

CYPHONIDÆ.

Helodes Latr.
ruficollis *Lec.*
  Lampyris ruficollis Say.
  Elodes fragilis Ziegler.

Scirtes Illiger.
centralis *Lec.*
  Attica centralis Say.
  ? Scirtes orbiculatus Fabr.
  Scirtes suturalis‖Ziegler.
  Scirtes lateralis Lec.

LYCIDÆ.

Calopteron Lap.
typicum *Lec.*
  Digrapha typica Newm.
  Digrapha discrepans Newm.
  Digrapha affinis Lec.
terminale *Lec.*
  Lycus terminalis Say.

Temnostoma Guér.
sanguinipennis *Lec.*
  Lycus sanguinipennis Say.

LAMPYRIDÆ.

Photinus Lap. (emend. Lac.)
  § **Ellychnia** Lec.
nigricans *Lec.*
  Lampyris nigricans Say.
  ? Lampyris obscura Fabr.
corrusca *Lec.*
  Lampyris corrusca Linn.
  §§ **Photinus** Lap.
pyralis *Lap.*
  Lampyris pyralis Linn.
  Lampyris centrata Say.
  Lampyris rosata Germ.
marginella *Lec.*
punctulata *Lec.*
obscurella *Lec.*

Photuris Lec.
pensylvanica *Lec.*
  Lampyris pensylvanica DeGeer.
  Lampyris versicolor Fabr.
divisa *Lec.*

TELEPHORIDÆ.

Chauliognathus Hentz
marginatus *Hentz.*
  Cantharis marginata Fabr.
  Cantharis ligata Say.
basalis *Lec.*, ante, 13.

Telephorus Geoffr.

collaris *Lec.*
bilineatus *Lec.*
    Cantharis bilineatus Say.
jactatus *Lec.*
    Cantharis jactata Say.
carolinus.
    Cantharis carolina Fabr.
luteicollis *Germ.*
    T. cinctellus Lec.
dichrous *Lec.*
flavipes *Lec.*

Podabrus Fischer.

rugosulus *Lec.*
punctulatus *Lec.*

Trypherus Lec.

latipennis *Lec.*
    Malthinus latipennis Germ.
    Molorchus marginalis Say.
    Malthinus marginalis Say.
    Lygerus latipennis Kiesenwetter.

MELYRIDÆ.

Collops Er.

bipunctatus *Er.*
    Malachius bipunctatus Say.
tricolor *Er.*
    Malachius tricolor Say.
punctatus *Lec.* Proc. Acad. Nat. Sc. VI, 164.
quadrimaculatus *Er.*
    Malachius 4-maculatus Fabr.
confluens *Lec.* Proc. Acad. Nat. Sc. VI, 164.
punctulatus *Lec.* ibid.

Ebæus Er.

morulus *Lec.* Proc. Acad. Nat. Sc. VI, 167.

Dasytes Fabr.

senilis *Lec.* Proc. Acad. Nat. Sc. VI, 170.

Byturus Fabr.

unicolor *Say.*

CLERIDÆ.

Cymatodera Gray.

undulata *Lec.*
    Tillus undulatus Say.
    Cymatodera longicollis Spin.
    Cymatodera Bosci Chevr.

Trichodes Herbst.

ornatus *Say.*
Nuttalli *Kirby.*

Clerus Geoffr.

analis *Say.*
cordifer *Lec.*
sphegeus *Fabr.*

Hydnocera Newm.

humeralis *Newman.*
    Clerus humeralis Germ.

Enoplium Latr.

pilosum *Latr.*
    Lampyris pilosa Forster.
    var. *Enoplium onustum* Say
    Enoplium marginatum||Say.
quadripunctatum *Say.*

Orthopleura Spin.

damicornis *Spin.*
    Tillus damicornis Fabr.
    Enoplium thoracicum Say.

Corynetes Fabr.

rufipes *Fabr.*
violaceus *Fabr.*

PTINIDÆ.

Dorcatoma Herbst.

simile *Say.*

BOSTRICHIDÆ

Bostrichus Geoffr. (emend. Lac.)

bicaudatus *Lec.*
    Apate bicaudatus Say.

TENEBRIONIDÆ.

Epitragus Latr.

canaliculatus *Say.*

Edrotes Lec.

rotundus *Lec.*
    Pimelia rotunda Say.

Trimytis Lec.

pruinosa *Lec.*

Pelecyphorus Sol.

sordidus *Lec.* Proc. Acad. Nat. Sc. VI, 446.

Euschides Lec.

convexa *Lec.*, ante, 14.
polita *Lec.*
    Asida polita Say.

Asida Latr.

opaca *Say.*

Pactostoma Lec.

anastomosis *Lec.* J. Ac. Nat. Sc. 2d ser. IV, 19.
Asida anastomosis Say.
Ologlyptus anastomosis Lac.

Eleodes Esch.

obscura *Lec.*
    Blaps obscura Say.
    ? *Blaps hispilabris* Say.
dispersa *Lec.* Proc. Acad. Nat. Sc. 1858, 182.
acuta *Lec.*
    Blaps acuta Say.
suturalis *Lec.*
    Blaps suturalis Say.
tricostata *Lec.*
    Blaps tricostata Say.
    Pimelia alternata Kirby.
sulcata *Lec.* Proc. Acad. Nat. Sc. VI, 67.
obsoleta *Lec.*
    Blaps obsoleta Say.
fusiformis *Lec.* Proc. Acad. Nat. Sc. 1858, 184.
extricata *Lec.*
    Blaps extricata Say.
carbonaria *Lec.*
    Blaps carbonaria Say.
nigrina *Lec.* Proc. Acad. Nat. Sc. 1858, 186.
Haydenii *Lec.* ibid. 1858, 186.
viator *Lec.* ibid. 1858, 188.

Promus Lec.

opacus *Lec.* Say's Ent. Writings, II, 155.
    Blaps opaca Say.

Embaphion Say.

muricatum *Say* (Akis).
contusum *Lec.* Journ. Acad. Nat. Sc. 2d ser. IV, 40.

Coniontis Esch.

obesa *Lec.*

Eusattus Lec.

reticulatus *Lec.*
    Zophosis reticulata Say.
convexus *Lec.*

Pedinus Latr.

? suturalis *Say* (fide Say).

Blapstinus Waterhouse.

interruptus *Lec.*
    Opatrum interruptum Say.
    Blapstinus æneolus Mels.
pratensis *Lec.*, ante, 15.
vestitus *Lec.*, ante, 15.

Centronopus Sol.

opacus *Lec.*, ante, 15.

Upis Fabr.

lævis *Oliv.*

Nyctobates Esch.

pensylvaniens *Lec.*
    Tenebrio pensylvanicus DeGeer.
    Upis chrysops Herbst.
barbatus *Lec.*
    Upis barbatus Knoch.

Boletophagus Illiger.

? cornutus *Fabr.*
    Opatrum cornutum Panz.
    Opatrum bifurcum Fabr.

Uloma Redt.

culinaris *Redt.*
    Tenebrio culinaris Linn.

Tenebrio Linn.

tenebrioides *Lec.*
    Helops tenebrioides Beauv.
    Tenebrio badipes Mels.

Paratenetus Spin.

punctatus *Spin.*

Adelina Dej.

pallida *Lec.*
    Pytho pallida Say.

Diaperis Geoffr.

hydni *Fabr.*

Platydema Lap.

excavatum *Lap.*

Allecula Fabr.

punctulata *Mels.*
obscura *Say.*

MELANDRYADÆ.

Eustrophus Fabr.

bicolor *Fabr.*

Melandrya Fabr.

labiata *Say.*

PEDILIDÆ.

Scraptia Latr.

plagiata *Mels.*
  S. americana Hald.

Stereopalpus Ferté.

guttatus *Lec.* Proc. Acad. Nat Sc. VII, 271.

ANTHICIDÆ.

Notoxus Geoffr.

anchora *Hentz.*
serratus *Lec.*
monodon *Ferté.*
  Anthicus monodon Fabr.
marginatus *Lec.*
subtilis *Lec.*

Anthicus Payk.

elegans *Ferté.*
rejectus *Lec.*
cervinus *Ferté.*
  A. bifasciatus||Say.
  A. terminalis Lec.
  A. bizonatus Ferté.

MORDELLIDÆ.

Mordella Fabr.

quadripunctata *Lec.*
  Anaspis 4-punctata Say.
insulata *Lec.*, ante, 16.
marginata *Mels.*

Mordellistena Costa.

æmula *Lec.*, ante, 16.
divisa *Lec.*, ante, 17.

RHIPIPHORIDÆ.

Emenadia Lap.

Sayi *Lec.*
  Rhipiphorus bicolor||Say.
limbatus *Lac.*
  Rhipiphorus limbatus Fabr.
pectinatus *Lec.*
  Rhipiphorus pectinatus Fabr.
  Rhipiphorus varicolor Gerst.

Myodites Latr.

scaber *Lec.* Proc. Acad. Nat. Sc. VI, 67.

MELOIDÆ.

Henous Hald.

confertus *Lec.* Proc. Acad. Nat. Sc. VI, 330.
  Meloe conferta Say.
  Henous lechanus Hald.

Lytta Fabr.

reticulata *Say.*
Nuttalli *Say.*
  var. *Cantharis fulgifer* Lec.
sphæricollis *Say.*
Engelmanni *Lec.* Proc. Acad. Nat. Sc. VI, 337.
  Pyrota Engelmanni Lec.
discoidea *Lec.* Proc. Acad. Nat. Sc. VI, 338.
pensylvanica *Lec.* ibid. VI, 339.
  Cantharis pensylvanica DeGeer.
  Lytta atrata Fabr.
ferruginea *Say.*
maculata *Say.*
conspersa *Lec.* Proc. Acad. Nat. Sc. VI, 340.
segmentata *Say* (segmenta).
albida *Say.*
  L. luteicornis Lec.
immaculata *Say.*
  ♂ *L. articularis* Say.
longicollis *Lec.* Proc. Acad. Nat. Sc. VI, 343.
Fabricii *Lec.* ibid.
  L. cinerea||Fabr.

Nemognatha Illiger.

bicolor *Lec.* Proc. Acad. Nat. Sc. VI, 345.
lurida *Lec.* ibid.
lutea *Lec.* ibid. VI, 346.
piezata *Lec.* ibid. VI, 347.
  Zonitis piezata Weber, Fabr.
  Zonitis vittata Fabr.
immaculata *Say.*
minima *Say.*

Zonitis Fabr.

atripennis *Lec.* Proc. Acad. Nat. Sc. VI, 349.
  Nemognatha atripennis Say.

ŒDEMERIDÆ.

Asclera Schmidt.

puncticollis *Hald.*
  Œdemera puncticollis Say.

ruficollis *Hald.*
 (Edemera ruficollis Say.
? vestita *Say* ((Edemera), fide Say.
 (an potius Stereopalpus.)

CURCULIONIDÆ.

Bruchus Linn.
discoideus *Say.*
and five others.

Spermophagus Steven.
Robiniæ *Sch.*
 Bruchus Robiniæ Fabr.

Cratoparis Sch.
lunatus *Sch.*
 Anthribus lunatus Fabr.
 Anthribus marmoreus Ol.

Attelabus Linn.
nigripes *Lec.*

Pterocolus Schönh.
ovatus *Schönh.*
 Attelabus ovatus Fabr.

Rhynchites Herbst.
bicolor *Herbst.*
 Attelabus bicolor Fabr.
æneus *Boheman.*
æratus *Say.*

Apion Herbst.
four species.

Ophryastes Schönh.
latirostris *Lec.* Proc. Acad. Nat. Sc. VI, 443.
ligatus *Lec.* ibid.
sulcirostris *Schönh.*
 Liparus sulcirostris Say.
vittatus *Schönh.* (infra).
 Liparus vittatus Say.

Epicærus Schönh.
? imbricatus (fide Say).
 Liparus imbricatus Say.
and four species? with four others of allied genera.

Platyomus Schönh.
auriceps *Schönh.*
 Curculio auricephalus Say.

Thylacites Germ.
microsus *Schönh.*
 T. microps Say.

Tanymecus Germ.
canescens *Schönh.*
confertus *Schönh.*
 T. confusus Say.

Cleonus Schönh.
pulverens *Lec.*, ante, 18.
trivittatus *Say.*
angularis *Lec.*, ante, 18.

Listroderes Schönh.
three species.

Lepyrus Germ.
geminatus *Say.*

Lithodus Germ.
humeralis *Germ.*
 Brachycerus humeralis Say.
 Thecesteraus humeralis Say.
rectus *Lec.* Proc. Acad. Nat. Sc. VIII, 18.
affinis *Lec.* Proc. Acad. Nat. Sc. VIII, 18.
rudis *Lec.* Proc. Acad. Nat. Sc. VIII, 18.
erosus *Lec.* Proc. Acad. Nat. Sc. VIII, 18.
longior *Lec.* Proc. Acad. Nat. Sc. VIII, 19.
morbillosus *Lec.* Proc. Acad. Nat. Sc. VIII, 19.

Lixus Fabr.
two species.

Erirhinus Schönh.
and allied genera 15 species.

Grypidius Schönh.
one species.

Balaninus Germ.
one species.

Piazorhinus Schönh.
scutellaris *Schönh.* Curc. III, 472; VII, 2, 352.
 Attelabus scutellaris Say.

Baridius Schönh.
seven species.

Centrinus Schönh.
two species.

Ceuthorhyncus Schüppel.
four species.

Rhyssematus Schönh.
lineaticollis *Schönh.*
 Rhynchænus lineaticollis Say.

Acalles Schönh.
three species.

Conotrachelus Latr.

posticatus *Schönh.*

Sphenophorus Schönh.

pulchellus *Schönh.*
cultirostris *Germ.*
compressirostris *Say.* (Calandra).
and seven others.

Cossonus Clairv.

subareatus *Schönh.*
and one other species.

Tomicus Latr.

pini *Harris.*
   Bostrichus pini Say.
caligraphus *Germ.*
   Bostrichus excsus Say.

CERAMBYCIDÆ.

Mallodon Serv.

dasystomus *Hald.*
   Prionus dasystomus Say.
cilipes *Hald.*
   Prionus cilipes Say.

Prionus Geoffr.

palparis *Say.*
imbricornis *Oliv.*
fissicornis *Hald.*
integer *Lec.*
emarginatus *Say.*

Criocephalus Muls.

productus *Lec.*
asperatus *Lec.*, ante, 19.
agrestis *Hald.*
   Callidium agreste Kirby.

Semanotus Muls.

brevilineus *Lec.*
   Callidium brevilineum Say.
   Physocnemum brevilineum Hald.

Callidium Fabr.

variabile *Fabr.*
amœnum *Say.*

Dryobius Lec.

sexfasciatus *Lec.*
   Callidium sexfasciatum Say.

Heliomanes Newman.

bimaculatus *Newman.*
   Molorchus bimaculatus Say.
   Molorchus affinis Lec.
   Heliomanes obscurus Lec. (err. typog.)

Eburia Serv.

quadrigeminata *Hald.*
   Stenocorus quadrigeminatus Say.

Elaphidion Serv.

simplicicolle *Hald.*
   E. pulverulentum ‡ Hald.
mucronatum *Newman.*
   Stenocorus mucronatus Say.
villosum *Dej.*
   Stenocorus villosus Fabr.
   Stenocorus putator Peck.

Eriphus Serv.

iguicollis *Lec.*
   Callidium ignicolle Say.
   Callidium sanguinicolle Germ.

Arhopalus Serv. (emend. Lec.)

fulminans *Serv.*
   Clytus fulminans Fabr.
charus *Lec.*
   Clytus charus Say.
pictus *Lec.*
   Cerambyx pictus Drury.
   Leptura Robiniæ Forster.
   Clytus flexuosus Fabr.

Rhopalophorus Serv.

longipes *Lec.*
   Stenocorus longipes Say.
   Tinopus longipes Lec.

Purpuricenus Serv.

humeralis *Dej.*
   Cerambyx humeralis Fabr.

Clytus Fabr.

scutellaris *Dej.*
   Callidium scutellare Oliv.
erythrocephalus *Fabr.*
undulatus *Say.*
   C. Sayi Lap.
   C. undatus Kirby.
capræa *Say.*
   C. elevatus Lap.

Acmæops Lec.

bivittata *Lec.*
   Leptura bivittata Say.
dorsalis *Lec.*, ante, 21.

Typocerus Lec.

sinuatus *Lec.*
   Leptura sinuata Newman.
   Stenura 8-notata Hald.

Leptura Linn.

cribripennis *Lec.*, ante, 21.
rubrica *Say.*

Monilema Say.

annulatum *Say.*

Plectrodera Lec.

scalator *Lec.*
   Lamia scalator Fabr.
   Lamia Belti Lec.

Oberea Muls.

perspicillata *Hald.*
oculaticollis *Lec.*
   Saperda oculaticollis Say.

Stenostola Muls.

pergrata *Lec.*
   Saperda pergrata Say.
gentilis *Lec.*
saturnina *Lec.*, ante, 21.

Amphionycha Lec.

ardens *Lec.*, ante, 22.

Tetrops Kirby.

canescens *Lec.*

Tetraopes Dalman.

tetraophthalmus *Harris.*
   Cerambyx tetraophthalmus Forster.
   Lamia tornator Fabr.
femoratus *Lec.*
annulatus *Lec.*

Saperda Fabr.

calcarata *Say*
   var. *S. adspersa* Lec.
mutica *Say.*
discoidea *Fabr.*
puncticollis *Say.*
   S. trigeminata Randall.
?inornata *Say* (fide Say).

7

Pogonocherus Latr.

parvulus *Lec.*

Psenocerus Lec.

supernotatus *Lec.*
   Clytus supernotatus Say.

Leptostylus Lec.

aculiferus *Lec.*
   Lamia aculifera Say.
   Amniscus marginellus Hald.

Liopus Serv.

cinereus *Lec.*

Acanthoderes Serv.

decipiens *Lec.*
   Ægomorphus decipiens Hald.

CHRYSOMELIDÆ.

Clythra Laichart.

laticlavia *Sch.*
   Chrysomela laticlavia Forster.
   Clythra obsita Fabr.

Babia Lac.

quadriguttata *Lac.*
   Clythra 4-guttata Oliv.

Coscinoptera Lac.

franciscana *Lec.*, ante, 22.

Cryptocephalus Geoffr.

lativittis *Germ.*
   C. geminatus Hald.
guttulatus *Oliv., Suffr.*
   C. lautus Newman.
mucoreus *Lec.*, ante, 23.
notatus *Oliv.*
   C. quadrimaculatus Say, Hald.
quadriguttulus *Suffrian.*
dispersus *Hald.*
venustus *Fabr., Hald.*
   C. ornatus Say.
   C. calidus Suffr.
leucomelas *Suffrian.*
fasciatus Say.
amatus *Hald.*
confluens *Say.*
viridis *Hald.*
   Monachus viridis Mels.
   ? *Cryptocephalus auratus* Fabr.

Pachybrachys Suffr.
hepaticus *Hald.*
  Cryptocephalus hepaticus Mels.
tridens *Mels.* /
mollis *Hald.*
viduatus *Suffr.*
  Cryptocephalus viduatus Fabr.
  Cryptocephalus bivittatus Say.
and four? other species.

Colaspis Fabr.
favosa *Say.*
and six? other species.

Metachroma Lec.
interruptum *Lec.*
  Colaspis interrupta Say.
pallidum *Lec.*
  Colaspis pallida Say.
  var. *Colaspis dubiosa* Say.

Paria Lec.
sexnotata *Lec.*
  Colaspis 6-notata Say.
quadrinotata *Lec.*
  Colaspis 4-notata Say.
aterrima *Lec.*
  Colaspis aterrima Oliv.
opacicollis *Lec.*, ante, 23.
pumila *Lec.*, ante, 23.

Heteraspis Lec.
nebulosa *Lec.*, ante, 23.
smaragdula *Lec.*, ante, 24.

Myochrous (+Chevr.).
denticollis *Lec.*
  Colaspis denticollis Say.
squamosus *Lec.*, ante, 24.

Chrysomela Linn.
scalaris *Lec.*
philadelphica *Linn.*
multipunctata *Say.*
  var. *C. verrucosa* Suffr. Ent. Zeit. 1858, 265.
exclamationis *Fabr.*
conjuncta *Rogers,* Proc. Acad. Nat. Sc. VIII, 34.
disrupta *Rogers,* ibid.
lunata *Fabr.*
  C. hybrida Say.
pulchra *Fabr.*
  var. *C. casta* Rogers, Pr. Ac. Nat. Sc. VIII, 33.
  C. lineata DeGeer.
  C. festiva Fabr.
incisa *Rogers,* Proc. Acad. Nat. Sc. VIII, 34.

praecelsa *Rogers,* Proc. Acad. Nat. Sc. VIII, 35.
auripennis *Say.*
basillaris *Say* (fide Say).
flavomarginata *Say.*
interrupta *Fabr.*
scripta *Fabr.*
obsoleta *Say.*
dissimilis *Say.*
formosa *Say.*

Doryphora Fabr.
10-lineata *Say.*
Rogersii *Lec.* Journ. Ac. Nat. Sc. 2d ser. IV, 26
trimaculata *Say.*
  Chrysomela trimaculata Linn.
  Chrysomela clivicollis Fabr.

Blepharida Rogers (+Chevr.).
rhois *Rogers.*
  Chrysomela rhois Forster.
  Chrysomela stolida Fabr.
  Altica virginica Fröhlich.

Œdionychis Latr.
gibbitarsa *Lec.*
  A. gibbitarsa Say.
scripticollis *Lec.*
  A. scripticollis Say.
lobata *Lec.*, ante, 24.

Haltica Illiger.
alternata *Illiger.*
  A. quinquevittata Say.
punctigera *Lec.*, ante, 24.
pluriligata *Lec.*, ante, 25.
collaris *Illiger.*
  Galleruca collaris Fabr.
cervicalis *Lec.*, ante, 25.
bimarginata *Say.*
subplicata *Lec.*, ante, 25.
punctipennis *Lec.*, ante, 25.
picta *Say.*
helxines *Illiger.*
  var. *A. nana* Say.
  Chrysomela helxines Linn.
erythropus *Lec.*
  Crepidodera erythropus Mels.

Glyptina Lec.
spuria *Lec.*, ante, 26.
lissotorquos *Lec.*, ante, 27.

Longitarsus Latr.
nigripalpis *Lec.*, ante, 26.
rubidus *Lec.*, ante, 26.

Chætoonema Steph.
denticulata *Lec.*
Haltica denticulata Illiger.
subviridis *Lec.*, ante, 27.

Cerotoma (⅃ Chevr.).
caminea *Fabr.* (Galleruca.)

Diabrotica (⅃ Chevr.).
thoracica *Mels.* (Calomicrus).
longicornis *Say* (Galleruca).
tricineta *Say* (Galleruca).
? atriventris *Say* (Galleruca), (fide Say).
? atripennis *Say* (Galleruca), (fide Say).

Adimonia Laich.
externa *Lec.*
Galleruca externa Say.

Galleruca Fabr.
dorsata *Say* (fide Say).
circumdata *Say* (fide Say).
and five other species.[1]

Hispa Fabr.
? collaris *Say* (fide Say).

Anoplitis Kirby.
scapularis *Lec.*
Hispa scapularis Oliv.
Hispa lateralis Say.
rosea *Lec.*
Hispa rosea Weber.
Hispa pallida Say.
Hispa Philemon Newman.

Microrhopala Chevr.
lætula *Lec.*, ante, 27.
cyanea *Lec.*
Hispa cyanea Say.
? *Hispa Hecate* Newman.

Chelymorpha Boheman.
Argus *Boh.*
Cassida Argus Herbst.
Cassida cribraria ‡ Oliv.
Imatidium 17-*punctatum* Say.

Cassida Herbst.
? unipunctata *Say.*
? ellipsis *Lec.*, ante, 28.

---

[1] These supposed species belong to the group of pubescent trivittate ones, and need more thorough investigation than can at present be made.

6-punctata *Fabr.*
C. bistripustulata Herbst.
nigripes *Oliv.*
atripes *Lec.*, ante, 28.

Coptocycla Boh.
pallida *Lec.*
Cassida pallida Herbst.
? *Coptocycla aurisplendens* Mann.
cruciata *Lec.*
Cassida cruciata DeG.
Cassida guttata Oliv.
Cassida signifer Herbst.
Coptocycla guttata Boh.
purpurata *Boh.*

COCCINELLIDÆ.

Anisosticta Chevr.
vittigera *Lec.*
Hippodamia vittigera Mann.
Naemia vittigera Muls.
episcopalis *Lec.*
Coccinella episcopalis Kirby.
Naemia episcopalis Muls.

Hippodamia Chevr.
glacialis *Muls.*
Coccinella glacialis Fabr.
Coccinella abbreviata Fabr.
Coccinella remota Weber.
13-punctata *Muls.*
Coccinella 13-*punctata* Linn.
Coccinella tibialis Say.
Leconti *Muls.*
convergens *Guér.*
Coccinella modesta Mels.
parenthesis *Lec.*
Coccinella parenthesis Say.
Coccinella tridens Kirby.
Adonia parenthesis Muls.

Coccinella Linn.
transversoguttata *Fald.*
C. 5-*notata* Kirby.
monticola *Muls.*
novemnotata *Herbst.*
abdominalis *Say.*
humeralis *Say* (fide Say).

Brachiacantha Chevr.
albifrons *Lec.*
Coccinella albifrons Say.
tau *Lec.*, ante, 28.
10-pustulata *Lec.*
Hyperaspis 10-*pustulata* Mels.

Hyperaspis Chevr.

vittigera *Lec.* Proc. Acad. Nat. Sc. VI, 133.
quadrivittata *Lec.* ibid. VI, 133.
elegans *Muls.*
  Coccinella undulata||Say.
pratensis *Lec.* Proc. Acad. Nat. Sc. VI, 134.

Œneis Muls.

pusilla *Lec.* Proc. Acad. Nat. Sc. VI, 135.

Scymnus Kug.

chatchas *Muls.*
  S. collaris Mels.
caudalis *Lec.*
? *S. creperus* Muls.

Sacium Lec.

lunatum *Lec.* Proc. Acad. Nat. Sc. VI, 144.

II. OF EASTERN NEW MEXICO.

CICINDELIDÆ.

Amblychila Say.

cylindriformis *Say.**
  A. Piccolominii Reiche.

Megacephala Latr.

virginica *Dej.**
  Cicindela virginica Linn.
carolina *Dej.*
  Cicindela carolina Linn.

Cicindela Linn.

pulchra *Say.**
purpurea *Oliv.**
  var. *C. Audubonii* Lec.
obsoleta *Say.**
cinctipennis *Lec.**
cuprascens *Lec.**
guttifera *Lec.*
punctulata *Fabr.**
  var. *C. micans* Fabr.
cumatilis *Lec.**
sedecimpunctata *Klug.*

CARABIDÆ.

Micrixys Lec.

distinctus *Lec.*
  Panagæus distinctus Hald.
  Eugnathus||*distinctus* Lec.

Helluomorpha Lap.

laticornis *Lap.**
  Helluo laticornis Dej.

Lachnophorus Dej.

elegantulus *Mann.**
  Tachypus mediosignatus Ménétr.

Apristus Chaud.

subsulcatus *Lec.*
  Dromius subsulcatus Dej.

Glycia Chaud.

viridicollis *Lec.**

Pristodactyla Dej.

dubia *Lec.* Proc. Acad. Nat. Sc. VII, 38.

Platynus Bon. (emend. Brullé.)

subcordatus *Lec.**
  Agonum erythropum||Kirby.
placidus *Lec.**
  Feronia placida Say.
  Agonum morosum Dej.

Evarthrus Lec.

substriatus *Lec.**
  Feronia (Molops) substriata Lec.

Pœcilus Bon.

scitulus *Lec.**

Amara Bon.

polita *Lec.**
fareta *Lec.* Proc. Acad. Nat. Sc. VII, 353.
musculus *Say.**
  Acrodon contempla Lec.
harpalina *Lec.* Proc. Acad. Nat. Sc. VII, 355.

Nothopus Lec.

zabroides *Lec.**
  Euryderus||*zabroides* Lec.
  ? *Amara grossa* Say.

Cratognathus Dej.

setosus *Lec.**
  Piosoma setosum Lec.
cordatus *Lec.* Trans. Am. Phil. Soc. X, 381.

Anisodactylus Dej.

rusticus *Dej.**
Harpalus rusticus Say.
Anisodactylus pinguis Lec.
Anisodactylus crassus Lec.
Anisodactylus gravidus Lec.
Anisodactylus tristis Dej.
chalceus *Lec.*, ante, 2.

Harpalus Latr.

impotens *Lec.* Journ. Ac. Nat. Sc. 2d ser. IV, 14.
amputatus *Say.**
H. Stephensii Kirby.
rotundicollis *Kirby.**
retractus *Lec.* Journ. Ac. Nat. Sc. 2d. ser. IV, 29.
H. impiger‖Lec. Proc. Ac. Nat. Sc. VII, 79.
fallax *Lec.*, ante, 2.
desertus *Lec.*, ante, 3.
oblitus *Lec.*, ante, 2.

Stenolophus Dej.

ochropezus *Dej.**
Feronia ochropeza Say.
dissimilis *Dej.**

Dicœlus Bon.

splendidus *Say.**

Chlænius Bon.

pensylvanicus *Say.**
C. vicinus Dej.
C. pubescens Harris.
laticollis *Say.**
C. diffinis Chaud.
sericeus *Say.**
Carabus sericeus Forster.
Chlænius perviridis Lec.

Pasimachus Bon.

validus *Lec.** Journ. Ac. Nat. Sc. 2d ser. IV, 14.
P. punctulatus‡Lec.
elongatus *Lec.**

Scarites Fabr.

subterraneus *Fabr.** (cum var.)

Clivina Latr.

bipustulata Dej.*
Scarites bipustulatus Fabr.
Scarites quadripustulatus Beauv.
Clivina quadripustulata Say.

Aspidoglossa Putz.

subangulata *Lec.**
Clivina crenata‡Dej.

Dyschirius subangulatus Chaud.
Dyschirius humeralis Chaud.
Aspidoglossa fraterna Putz.
Aspidoglossa vicina Putz.
Clivina bipustulata‡Say.

Bembidium Latr.

coxendix *Say.**
Odontium coxendix Lec.
dorsale *Say.**
pictum *Lec.**

Calosoma Fabr.

scrutator *Fabr.**
externum *Lec.**
Carabus externus Say.
Calosoma longipenne Dej.

DYTISCIDÆ.

Hydroporus Clairv.

striatellus *Lec.*
vilis *Lec.*

Anisomera Brullé.

cordata *Lec.*

Colymbetes Clairv.

binotatus *Harris.**
C. maculicollis Aubé.

Cybister Curtis.

fimbriolatus *White,** Brit. Mus. Cat. 5.
Dytiscus fimbriolatus Say.
Cybister dissimilis Aubé.
ellipticus *Lec.*

HYDROPHILIDÆ.

Hydrophilus Geoffr.

triangularis *Say.**
H. lugubris Motsch.
Stethoxus subsulcatus Lec. Pr. Ac. VII, 221.
lateralis *Fabr., Lec.** Pr. Ac. Nat. Sc. VII, 367.
ellipticus *Lec.* ibid. VII, 368.

STAPHYLINIDÆ.

Staphylinus Linn.

villosus *Grav.**

Philonthus Leach.

two species.

SILPHIDÆ.

Necrophorus Fabr.
mediatus Fabr.*

Silpha Linn.
peltata Lec.*
  Scarabæus peltatus Catesby.
  Silpha americana Linn.
lapponica Herbst.*
  S. caudata Say.
  S. tuberculata Germ.
  S. californica Mann.
  Oiceoptoma granigerum Chevr.
truncata Say.*
ramosa Say.*

NITIDULIDÆ.

Carpophilus Leach.
pallipennis Lec.*
  C. floralis Er. Germ. Zeitschr. IV, 261.
  Cercus pallipennis Say.

Nitidula Fabr.
ziczac Say.*

CUCUJIDÆ.

Læmophlœus Er.
biguttatus Mels.*
  Cucujus biguttatus Say.
  Læmophlœus bisignatus Guér.

Nausibius Redt.
dentatus Redt.* Fauna Austr. 999.
  Lyctus dentatus Fabr.
  Silvanus dentatus Say.

DERMESTIDÆ.

Dermestes Linn.
marmoratus Say.*
fasciatus Lec. Proc. Acad. Nat. Sc. VII, 107.

Attagenus Latr.
spurcus Lec. Proc. Acad. Nat. Sc. VII, 109.
  ? A. cylindricornis Say.
dichrous Lec. Proc. Acad. Nat. Sc. VII, 110.

Trogoderma Latr.
pusillum Lec. Proc. Acad. Nat. Sc. VII, 111.

PARNIDÆ.

Helichus Er.
foveatus Lec. Proc. Acad. Nat. Sc. VI, 43.
æqualis Lec. Proc. Acad. Nat. Sc. VII, 81.

SCARABÆIDÆ.

Strategus Hope.
Julianus Burm., Lamell. III, 133.

Aphonus Lec.
tridentatus Lec.* Proc. Acad. Nat. Sc. VIII, 22.
  Scarabæus tridentatus Say.

Ligyrus Burm.
gibbosus Lec.* Proc. Acad. Nat. Sc. VIII, 20.
  Scarabæus gibbosus DeGeer.
  Podalgus variolosus Burm.

Phileurus Latr.
valgus Dej.,* Burm., Lamell. III, 160.
  Geotrupes valgus Fabr.
  Phileurus castaneus Hald.

Cremastochilus Knoch.
saucius Lec.* Journ. Ac. Nat. Sc. 2d ser. IV, 16.

Euryomia Burm. (emend. Lac.)
melancholica Lac.* Gen. Col. III, 528.
  Cetonia melancholica Gory.
Kernii Lac. ibid.
  Euphoria cernii Hald.
Clarkii Lac. ibid.
  Euphoria Clark ii Lec. Proc. Acad. Nat. Sc.
  VI, 414.

Allorhina Burm. (emend. Lac.)
mutabilis? Lac. Gen. Col. III, 497.
  Cotinis mutabilis Burm., Lamell. I, 255.
  Gymnetis mutabilis Gory.

Anomala Samouelle.
varians Burm.*
  Melolontha varians Fabr.

Strigoderma Burm.
arboricola Burm.*
  Melolontha arboricola Fabr.

Polyphylla Harris.
decemlineata Lec.*
  Melolontha 10-lineata Say.

Thyce Lec.
squamicollis *Lec.* J. Ac. Nat. Sc. 2d ser. III, 232.

Laehnosterna Hope.
lanceolata *Lec.**
Melolontha lanceolata Say.
Tostegoptera lanceolata Blanchard.

Dichelonyoha Kirby.
sulcata *Lec.* Journ. Acad. Nat. Sc. 2d ser. III, 281.

Hoplia Illiger.
laticollis *Lec.* Journ. Ac. Nat. Sc. 2d ser. III, 284.

Trox Fabr.
alternans *Lec.** Proc. Acad. Nat. Sc. VII, 211.

Canthon Illiger.
praticola *Lec.*,* ante, 10.

BUPRESTIDÆ.

Psiloptera Sol. (emend. Lac.)
Woodhousei *Lec.**
Dicerca Woodhousei Lec.
var. *Psiloptera vulens* Lec.

Ancylochira Esch.
confluens *Lec.**
Buprestis confluens Say.
alternans *Lec.* Trans. Am. Phil. Soc. XI, 207.
subornata *Lec.* Trans. Am. Phil. Soc. XI, 208.

Melanophila Esch.
miranda *Lec.*
Phaenops mirandus Lec. Proc. Acad. VII, 83.

Anthaxia Esch.
retifera *Lec.* Trans. Am. Phil. Soc. XI, 215.
imperfecta *Lec.* Trans. Am. Phil. Soc. XI, 215.

Chrysobothris Esch.
quadrilineata *Lec.* Trans. Am. Phil. Soc. XI, 233.
cuprascens *Lec.* Trans. Am. Phil. Soc. XI, 233.

Acmæodera Esch.
variegata *Lec.* Proc. Acad. Nat. Sc. VI, 67.
mixta *Lec.** Trans. Am. Phil. Soc. XI, 227.

ELATERIDÆ.

Cratonychu Er.
exuberans *Lec.* Trans. Am. Phil. Soc. X, 477.

TELEPHORIDÆ.

Silis Charp.
difficilis *Lec.*

Telephorus Geoffr.
fidelis *Lec.*

MELYRIDÆ.

Collops Er.
bipunctatus *Er.**
Malachius bipunctatus Say.

Dasytes Fabr.
erythropus *Lec.* Proc. Acad. Nat. Sc. VI, 171.

CLERIDÆ.

Cymatodera Gray.
longicornis *Lec.*

Trichodes Herbst.
ornatus *Say.**

Clerus Geoffr.
mexicanus *Spin.*
moestus *Klug.*
C. truncatus Lec.

Corynetes Fabr.
rufipes *Fabr.**
violaceus *Fabr.**

PTINIORES.

Niptus Boield.
ventriculus *Lec.*, ante, 13.

Trypopitys Redt.
punctatus *Lec.*, ante, 13.

TENEBRIONIDÆ.

Epitragus Latr.
canaliculatus *Say.**

Eurymetopon Esch.
abnorme *Lec.*
atrum? *Lec.*

Pactostoma Lec.

anastomosis Lec.*
Asida anastomosis Say.

Pelecyphorus Sol.

sordidus Lec.* Proc. Acad. Nat. Sc. VI, 46.

Euschides Lec.

convexicollis Lec. Proc. Acad. Nat. Sc. VII, 224.
obovata Lec.
convexa Lec.,* ante, 14.
polita Lec.
Asida polita Say.

Asida Latr.

opaca Say.
Euschides opaca Lec.

Zopherus Gray.

concolor Lec.

Eleodes Esch.

obscura Lec.*
Blaps obscura Say.
? *Blaps hispilabris* Say.
acuta Lec.*
Blaps acuta Say.
tricostata Lec.*
Blaps tricostata Say.
Pimelia alternata Kirby.
gracilis Lec. Proc. Acad. Nat. Sc. 1858, 184.
sponsa Lec. ibid. 184.
caudifera Lec. ibid. 184.
obsoleta Lec.*
Blaps obsoleta Say.
debilis Lec. Proc. Acad. Nat. Sc. 1858, 185.
extricata Lec.*
Blaps extricata Say.
carbonaria Lec.*
Blaps carbonaria Say.
nigrina Lec. Proc. Acad. Nat. Sc. 1858, 186.

Embaphion Say.

contusum Lec. J. Acad. Nat. Sc. 2d ser. IV, 40.*

Eusattus Lec.

reticulatus Lec.*
Zophosis reticulata Say.

Blapstinus Dej.

pratensis Lec.,* ante, 15.

Nyctobates Esch.

pensylvanicus Lec.*
Tenebrio pensylvanicus Knoch.
Upis chrysops Herbst.

Xystropus Sol.

pinguis Lec., ante, 16.

Cistela Fabr.

sericea Say.*

MELOIDÆ.

Meloe Linn.

sublævis Lec. Proc. Acad. Nat. Sc. VII, 84.
parvulus Hald. Proc. Acad. Nat. Sc. VI, 404.
M. parvus Hald.

Lytta Fabr.

biguttata Lec. Proc. Acad. Nat. Sc. VI, 332.
maculata Say.*
costata Lec. Proc. Acad. Nat. Sc. VII, 84.
longicollis Lec.* Proc. Acad. Nat. Sc. VI, 343.
Fabricii Lec.* Proc. Acad. Nat. Sc. VI, 343.
L. cinerea Fabr., Harris.

Tetraonyx Latr.

fulva Lec. Proc. Acad. Nat. Sc. VI, 344.

Nemognatha Illiger.

nigripennis Lec. Proc. Acad. Nat. Sc. VI, 347.
cribraria Lec. Proc. Acad. Nat. Sc. VI, 348.
immaculata Say.*

Zonitis Fabr.

flavida Lec. Proc. Acad. Nat. Sc. VI, 349
rufa Lec. Proc. Acad. Nat. Sc. VII, 85.

ŒDEMERIDÆ.

Calopus Fabr.

angustus Lec.

Asclera Schmidt.

obscura Lec. Proc. Acad. Nat. Sc. VII, 21.

Mycterus Oliv.

concolor Lec. Proc. Acad. Nat. Sc. VI, 235.

CURCULIONIDÆ.

Bruchus Linn.

one species.

Ophryastes Schönh.

tuberosus Lec. Proc. Acad. Nat. Sc. VI, 443.
vittatus Schönh.*
Liparus vittatus Say.

Tanymecus Germ.
lautus *Lec.* Proc. Acad. Nat. Sc. VII, 85.

Sitones Germ.
scissifrons *Say.*

Cleonus Schönh.
lutulentus *Lec.*, ante, 18.

Anthonomus Germ.
one species.

Baridius Schönh.
one species.

Cossonus Clairv.
one species.

Tomicus Latr.
pini *Harris.**
Bostrichus pini Say.
caligraphus *Germ.**
Bostrichus exesus Say.

CERAMBYCIDÆ.

Derobrachus Serv.
geminatus *Lec.* Proc. Acad. Nat. Sc. VI, 233.

Prionus Geoffr.
curvatus *Lec.*, ante, 19.
palparis *Say.**
fissicornis *Hald.**

Criocephalus Muls.
asperatus *Lec.*, ante, 19.

Elaphidion Serv.
villosum *Hald.**
Stenocorus villosus Fabr.
Stenocorus putator Peck.
debile *Lec.* Proc. Acad. Nat. Sc. VI, 442.

Eriphus Serv.
? ignicollis *Say* (Callidium).*
Callidium sanguinicolle Germ.
? rutilans *Lec.* (Arhopalus).

Arhopalus Serv. (emend. Lec.)
pictus *Lec.**
Cerambyx pictus Drury.
Leptura Robiniæ Forster.
Clytus flexuosus Fabr.

8

Tylosis Lec.
maculatus *Lec.*

Stenaspis Dupont.
solitaria *Lec.**
Cerambyx solitarius Say.
Smileceras solitarium Lec.

Rhagium Fabr.
lineatum *Schönh.**
Stenocorus lineatus Oliv.

Leptura Linn.
auripilis *Lec.*

Monilema Say.
appressum *Lec.*

Monohammus Latr.
clamator *Lec.*

Stenostola Muls.
pergrata *Lec.**
Saperda pergrata Say.

Tetraopes Dalm.
canescens *Lec.*

Saperda Fabr.
concolor *Lec.*

Ædilis Serv.
spectabilis *Lec.*, ante, 22.

CHRYSOMELINÆ.

Lema Fabr.
trivirgata *Lec.*, ante, 22.

Urodera Lac.
crucifera *Lac.* Mon. Chrysom. II, 454.

Cryptocephalus Geoffr.
confluens *Say.**
one species.

Colaspis Fabr.

Myochrous Chevr.
denticollis *Lec.**
Eumolpus denticollis Say.

Chrysomela Linn.
auripennis *Say** (cum var. cœrulea).
interrupta *Fabr.**
formosa *Say.**

Œdionychis Latr.

Ingens Lec., ante, 24.

Haltica Fabr.

alternata Illiger.*
H. quinquevittata Say.
semicarbonata Lec., ante, 25.
ambiens Lec., ante, 25.
obliterata Lec., ante, 26.
punctipennis Lec.,* ante, 25.
torquata Lec., ante, 26.
bitæniata Lec., ante, 26.

Luperus Geoffr.

rufipes Lec., ante, 27.

Galleruca Geoffr.

one species.

Microrhopala Chevr.

cyanea Lec.*
Hispa cyanea Say.
? Hispa Hecate Newman.

Cassida Herbst.

sexpunctata Fabr.*
C. bistripustulata Herbst.

EROTYLIDÆ.

Erotylus Fabr.

Boisduvalii Chevr.

COCCINELLIDÆ.

Anisosticta Chevr.

vittigera Lec.*
Hippodamia vittigera Mann.

Hippodamia Chevr.

Lecontii Muls.*
convergens Guérin.*
H. modesta Mels.

Coccinella Linn.

monticola Mels.*

Psyllobora Chevr.

vigintimaculata Say.*

Brachiacantha Chevr.

albifrons Lec.*
Coccinella albifrons Say.

Epilachna Chevr.

corrupta Muls. Cocc. 815.

PUBLISHED BY THE SMITHSONIAN INSTITUTION,

WASHINGTON CITY,

DECEMBER, 1859.

PL.I.

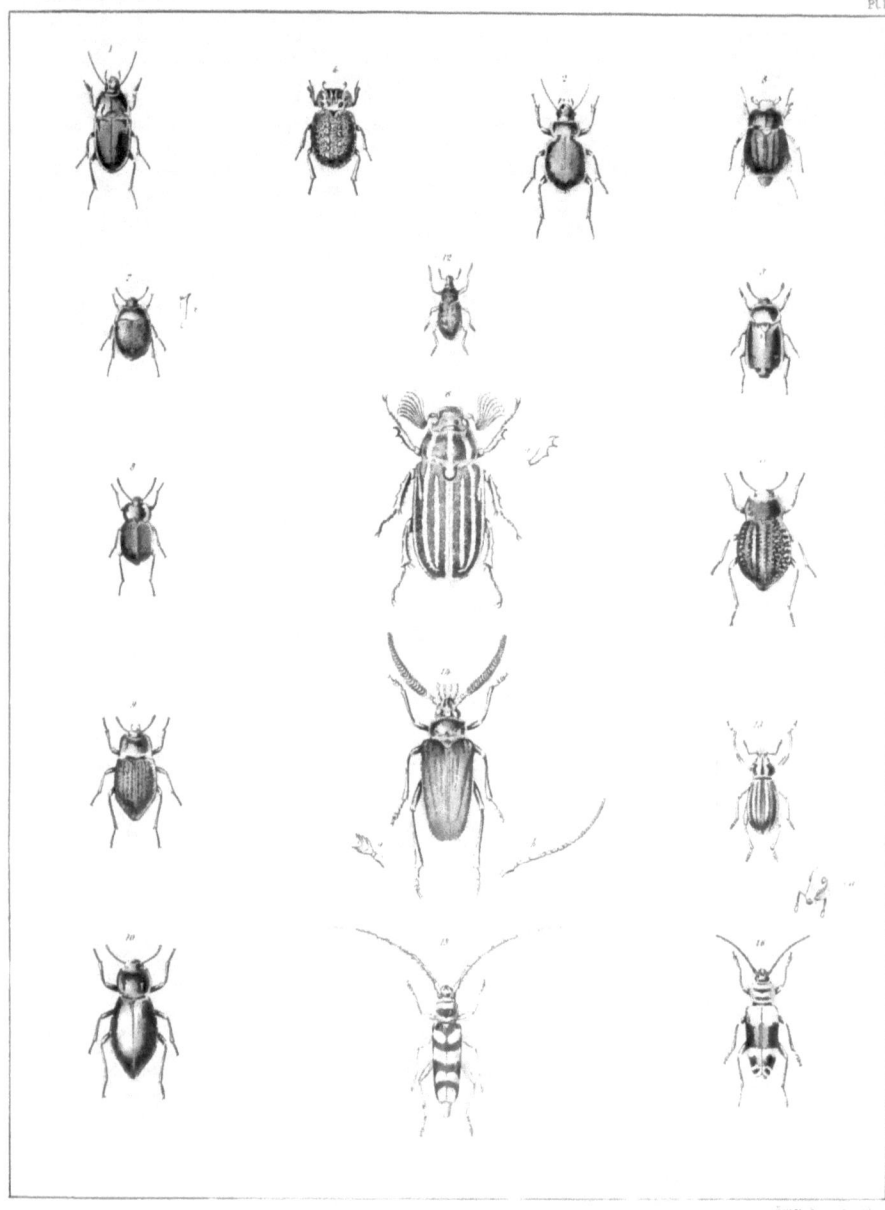

1 DICAELUS LAEVIPENNIS
2 CALOSOMA LUXATUM
3 SILPHA TRUNCATA
4 OMORGUS SCUTELLARIS

5
6
7
8 EMBAPHION PRAELOID

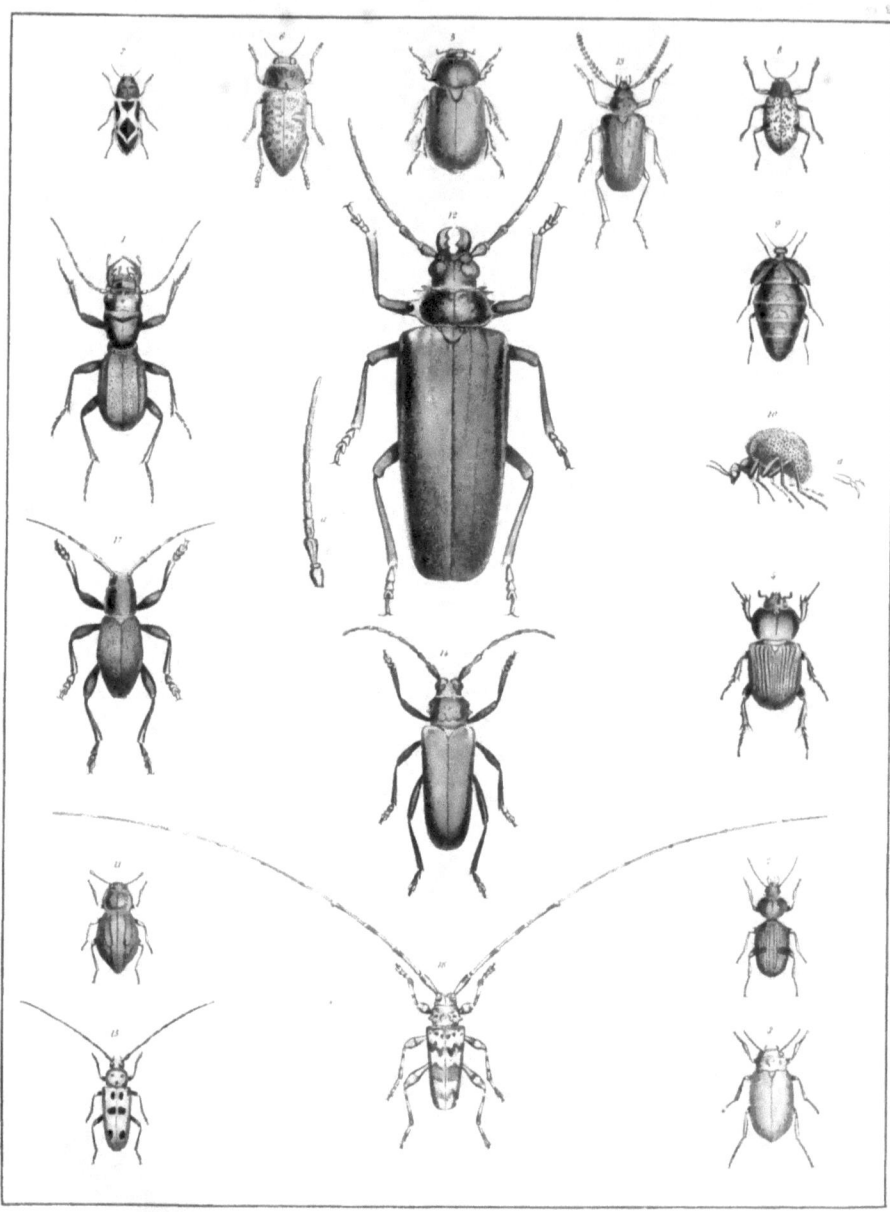